LEAD RECKONING

LEAD RECKONING

RAY HOGAN

THORNDIKE
C H I V E R S

LIBRARY OF CONGRESS CATALOGING-IN-PUBLICATION DATA

Hogan, Ray, 1908–
    Lead reckoning / by Ray Hogan.
       p. cm. — (Thorndike Press large print Western)
    ISBN-13: 978-0-7862-9954-6 (hardcover : alk. paper)
    ISBN-10: 0-7862-9954-1 (hardcover : alk. paper)
    1. Large type books. I. Title.
PS3558.O3473L4 2007
813'.54—dc22   2007030757

BRITISH LIBRARY CATALOGUING-IN-PUBLICATION DATA AVAILABLE

Published in 2007 in the U.S. by arrangement with Golden West Literary Agency.
Published in 2008 in the U.K. by arrangement with The Golden West Literary Agency.

U.K. Hardcover: 978 1 405 64352 8 (Chivers Large Print)
U.K. Softcover: 978 1 405 64353 5 (Camden Large Print)

Printed in the United States of America on permanent paper
10 9 8 7 6 5 4 3 2 1

LEAD RECKONING

CHAPTER ONE

For Jim Strike it was like coming to the end of a long trail, measured not only in miles but also in years.

He rode slowly across the lush Tenkiller country; a vast, beautiful land lying just north of the Mexican border in New Mexico territory. A curious feeling of ease and contentment flowed through his lank body as his deep-set eyes drifted back and forth over the long, rolling prairies, the low hills. It was as he had remembered — broad, quiet, rich — ideal for the cattle ranch he had dreamed a lifetime of owning.

It had been more than a journey of distance. There had been restless, fiddlefooted years while he wandered the far flung Territories. He had seen the great spreads of other men, had looked upon their grasslands and their herds of grazing cattle while the relentless claws of ambition dug deeper and deeper into his hungering soul. But for him it was slow going. A cowboy made small money. And then the war had come and he threw in with Canby to do his part, finding himself later in the larger theater of battle along the Potomac.

It was during that period he met Arlie Silvershell. In the tall, yellow-haired Missourian, five years his senior, he discovered a kindred spirit, one also consumed by a remorseless desire to one day own his own spread. They had formed a pact; should they live they would meet after the war, pool their efforts and resources and fulfill their hopes.

After Appomattox they had kept in contact by occasional letters while each labored to complete his part of the bargain — Arlie to claim Tenkiller Valley for the site of their ranch, begin the construction of necessary buildings and make what money he could; Strike to work until he had accumulated at least a thousand dollars, that money to go for an original herd. It had taken a full five years but now, at last, the time of consummation was at hand. The past was the past. The time of yearning was over and only the future counted. All that mattered now was the partnership with Arlie and the success of their ranch.

He rode on, seeing the plains green up

gradually but definitely as he drew nearer the hills. The spring had assuredly been a wet one and the land looked good with short grass spreading everywhere like a pale, emerald froth. It was magnificent country, rolling away as far as the eye could see with a clean, clear sky cupped over it like a huge, protective canopy. Quail and dove were plentiful, hurtling up and away at his approach. And once he saw a band of antelope racing off into the sun, their golden coats glistening brightly, white rump patches flashing.

In Arlie's last letter, which had caught up with him in Montana, there had been mention and promise of a surprise that was awaiting him. Strike wondered about it all during the lengthy ride from the north. And he had wondered, too, about Arlie Silvershell. Had he changed much? Was he still the same easy-going, laughing man, friendly to an extreme on the one hand and, paradoxically, unchained violence when aroused, on the other?

There had been times during the war, Jim Strike thought, when Arlie might have won a battle single-handed, so wild and destructive was his anger. And there were the moments when he was gentle and kind as a woman. What would he be like now, after five years? Likely he will have altered little, Strike decided. He would be the same Arlie, the identical man who had carried him tenderly off the battlefield at Gettysburg under the withering fire of enemy rifles one day and, on the very next, been the wild, raging demon who had led a patrol to victory up a seemingly impossible slope. Within himself, a man never really changes much. Their partnership would work; it would be a success. He, Jim Strike, would make it so.

A flight of summer ducks swept by overhead, their wings swishing hurriedly through the hot, June air. Strike watched them lift suddenly and veer off, to glide toward some distant pond or wider section of the creek which carved its way along the floor of the valley.

The conformation of Tenkiller Valley became more apparent as he drew nearer. It lay north and south, its opening marked by rocky bluffs, spaced some eight miles or so apart. *Shaped like a bullet,* he thought. Blunt at its opening to the south, tapering to a point ten miles or better in the north. An ideal location for a ranch. He had realized that when he had first set eyes on it, during that time he was with Canby's troops. There was good grazing land both within and beyond the valley proper. A man could run

10

stock on the upper plateaus during the summer months, bring them down to lower ground in the winter where they would be protected from the weather.

He reached the mouth of the valley and swung northward. A well defined wagon road lay before him, threading its way through a thick stand of tamarack. He turned his bay horse onto it and settled slackly into his saddle. It would not be much farther now. Another hour or so. Far ahead he watched a column of blue smoke trickling upward into the cloudless sky. That would be the ranch — their ranch, his and Arlie's.

The bay rounded a curve in the road, halted abruptly. Strike came upright in the saddle, his nerves singing with a sudden warning of danger.

Two riders were before him, blocking his way with drawn guns. One was a tall, heavily built man wearing the clothing of a Mexican *vaquero,* the other a blond American. Each wore a bandana mask across his face, revealing only the eyes. Jim Strike watched them narrowly, waiting. He heard other sounds then and knew more riders had slipped up behind him.

"Up with your hands, *señor,*" the *vaquero,*

evidently the leader, said in an accented voice.

Strike stared briefly at the threatening pistols and slowly lifted his arms. "What's this all about?"

"A matter of business," the outlaw said evenly. "Get down from the horse."

In the tense hush Strike climbed from the bay. He watched as the blond dismounted and moved cautiously toward him. It was a hold-up. It could hardly be anything else. He was unknown in the area; he would have no enemies with other purpose in mind. The outlaw circled him. He felt the slight change of weight at his hip as the man lifted his gun from its holster and tossed it aside.

"If you're looking for money," Strike said coolly, "You're wasting time."

The *vaquero* laughed, the sound dry and muffled. "We shall see, *señor.* You will keep your hands up high while my friend Chris has the look."

Strike's muscles bunched. He was carrying his money, nearly fourteen hundred dollars, on his person. It was in two small pouches sewed inside the legs of his boots, all in currency and gold coin. Likely they would never think to look in such a place but he was unwilling to take the chance. His future, and that of Arlie Silvershell, depended on the stake he was to provide. Too many years had gone into the making of it. He could not lose it now.

He felt the blond outlaw's hands explore about his waist, seeking a belt. The man was behind him, offering no opportunity to act. And there were the others, the ones who had closed in after he had been halted. The outlaw's hands dug into his pockets, came out with the few loose coins he carried for food and trail necessities.

"The hat," the *vaquero* suggested. "Look inside the hat band."

The blond thrust the coins into his own shirt pocket and reached for Strike's wide-brimmed hat. In that moment Jim acted. He brought his arms down in a quick, sledging blow. The rock-hard heels of his hands drove into the outlaw's neck, near the shoulder. The blond yelled and sagged. Strike seized him, spun him about. Holding him as a shield, he stepped back against the bay horse.

The *vaquero* laughed again. "You are a fast one, *señor*. But for little cause. Behind you are others." He lifted his glance, nodded. "Help your friend, Red."

The blond had begun to squirm, trying to break free of Strike's powerful grasp. He wrestled against the tall rider, curses stream-

13

ing from his lips, but he made little headway. Strike held on, striving to keep his own back against the bay as a protective measure but the gelding, alarmed by the scuffling, kept moving away. Suddenly, a hard blow to the side of his head sent lights bursting before his eyes.

His grip about the man called Chris relaxed for a second. The blond wrenched free, wheeled. He swung a wide right at Strike. Jim, his head clearing fast, ducked and drove a hard left straight into the man's face. The blond stopped dead, a howl of pain bursting from his lips. Strike lunged at the man, outstretched fingers reaching for the outlaw's gun. Something smashed into the side of his head again, rocked his senses. Hands jerked at his arms, drew them back, pinned them behind him. He shook his head savagely, trying to clear away the webs that clouded it. He saw the blond outlaw move in fast, fists upraised, heard him speak.

"Hold him, Red! I'm goin' to teach him a thing or two!"

The first blow caught Strike on the chin and drove his head back. The second went into his belly, exploding his breath in a gusty blast. Strike struggled to pull his arms free, to cover and protect himself, to fight back. He was helpless. But he hung on grimly, desperately seeking a way to break away. And then suddenly everything went black.

He came to. He was lying in the dusty roadway, the full glare of the sun beating down upon him. He felt sick and his head throbbed dully — and he was not alone. Some inner instinct warned him of that fact. The outlaws were still at hand. He opened his eyes to narrow slits. There were five of them, he saw. They had dismounted and squatted in the shade of the tamarack.

"There ain't no big money on him," the blond said at that moment. Above his mask, a dark discoloration was deepening below his right eye where Strike's fist had driven home. "You reckon he's the right man?"

The *vaquero* shrugged. "I am sure. This is the day he was to come. And there have been no other riders to cross the flats."

"Well," the blond said, "somebody's sure got somethin' wrong. He ain't carryin' no thousand dollars."

One of the others, a thin dark man, pushed his hat to the back of his head, grinned. "He sure was carryin' somethin' else though, weren't he, Calloway? Proved it by that eye of your'n!"

The blond grunted and tugged at his mask. The *vaquero* said, "A curly wolf, that one. And no fool. He likely sent the money by mail, on the stage."

"Bound to be the way of it," the rider said and got to his feet. "Reckon there ain't no use settin' out here in this sun. You goin' back to Largo?"

The others got to their feet. The *vaquero* said, "You go. I will come later." He threw a sharp glance at Strike.

"What about him?" Calloway asked.

The Mexican moved his shoulders slightly. "He sleeps. When he awakens, we shall be gone. *Adios,*" he added, and turned to his horse.

Strike watched the others follow to their mounts. They swung to the saddle and wheeled away, the four of them doubling back along the route he had just covered, the fifth, the *vaquero,* riding on into the valley. When he was certain they were well on their way, he sat up. Pain flooded his head but he ignored it, struggled to his feet. He located his gun and thrust it back into its holster, then took up the reins of the gelding and started for the small stream he could see glittering to his left. He reached it, dropped flat on the soft, sandy bank and buried his head in the cold water. It swept his breath away but his mind began to clear immediately and it made him feel much better. After a minute he settled back, resting himself against the trunk of a small cotton-wood tree.

His money was safe. The conversation of the outlaws and the slight pressure of the pouches against his legs told him that. They had not thought to look inside his boots, which was fortunate. But there was something else, something that disturbed him deeply. They had known all about the money! They had expected to find it on his person. How could that be possible?

He had written Arlie that he was coming, of course, even stated the day he would arrive. But he had said nothing about the money, merely stating that he was ready to begin. It was logical to believe others might see and read the letter — but they could know nothing about the thousand dollars he would be carrying. Yet the *vaquero* and the four riders with him were aware of it, even the exact amount! Arlie, of course, might have mentioned it at some time, but he doubted that. Not the exact amount, in any event.

Strike rose and swung onto the bay, his dark, windburned face quiet in study. For a long minute he sat motionless on the saddle, his wide, square-cut shoulders silhouetted against the skyline as he puzzled over the strangeness of it all. Finally, giving it up, he shrugged, touched the gelding with his spurs and guided him back to the road. He would tell Arlie about it. Maybe he would have some ideas on the matter.

It was near noon with the sun almost straight overhead. He rode out of a thick stand of timber that girdled the valley like a belt of solid green and halted on the rim of a small bowl. The scene that sprawled out before him almost took his breath away. Here, beyond the shadow cup, the valley ended, the steep ragged walls of a box canyon rising abruptly to form its termination. Lying in a flat meadow a short distance in front of the bluffs, was a scatter of buildings; a long ranch house, two or three barns, several minor structures and pole corrals.

Water sparkled from the east side of the canyon, cascaded down in a silvery, shimmering fall. It formed a fair-sized creek which raced for the ranch house, disappeared behind it briefly, appeared again in a flashing strip that hurried on down the valley a short distance to empty into a small pond. A new creek drained away from that diminutive lake and snaked its way on down the broad swale — the same stream, Strike realized, that he had crossed several times on the journey up from the buttes.

It was a neat, practical layout. Arlie had

done well. He saw the back door of the main house swing back and a portly Mexican woman, obviously the cook, emerged and waddled towards a chicken yard a short distance away. Two or three dozen fowl scrambled frantically against the wire to greet her. Beyond the enclosure he could see a garden patch, green with growing vegetables.

His pulse quickening with anticipation and pride, he urged the bay forward, pointing him for the hitching rack that stood before the main house. He pulled up, stopped. He pushed his hat to the back of his head, and, still in the saddle, called out.

"Hello, the house!"

A voice from somewhere deep within the structure answered. A moment later the screen door came open. A tall, powerfully built man with hair the color of sunflowers stepped out onto the porch. It was Arlie. Older, somewhat heavier, but unquestionably Arlie Silvershell.

He threw a bewildered glance at Strike, squinting a little from the sun, while words of some sort formed on his lips. And then he straightened. His wide mouth split into a grin and he came off the porch in a single bound.

"Jim! Jim Strike! Been expecting you!"

He grasped Strike's outstretched hand, pulled him off the bay gelding. He clapped Strike hard on the shoulder.

"Man and boy, I'm glad to see you! How d'you like the way the place looks? Bet you didn't expect to see things this far along, eh? You had anything to eat? Let's go inside and I'll have the cook fix you up."

Strike did not move. He remained where he stood, a slow grin on his lips. Arlie had not changed in the slightest. Being partners with him in a venture they both had long dreamed of was going to be pure pleasure. Motion beyond Arlie, at the door of the house, caught his attention. He lifted his glance. A girl, tall, well formed and with a wealth of pale, golden hair stepped out onto the gallery. Her face was finely carved with high cheekbones and delicate features and her eyes, definitely slanted, appeared to be green.

Silvershell, noting Strike's shift of attention, whirled about. He saw the girl, caught Strike's arm and dragged him toward the porch.

"Remember that surprise I was tellin' you about? Well, here it is! Gone and got myself married! Got me the prettiest woman in the whole blasted country! Jim, this is my wife, Angelina!"

Arlie stepped up on the porch, moved in behind the girl. He threw his arms around her, hugged her close. Standing thus, he was a full head and shoulders taller than she.

"Angelina, this is the man we've been waiting for. This is my old sidekick, Jim Strike!"

Strike removed his hat. He offered his hand. Angelina accepted it slowly. There was a faint smile on her full, perfectly-shaped lips, but the welcome ended there. In her eyes he saw only hostility.

CHAPTER TWO

Jim Strike felt the chill of Angelina's greeting settle over him, lower his spirits, dampen his hopes. He fell back a step. Arlie, unaware of it all, laughed his big, booming laugh.

"See, Jim? Didn't I tell you I had me the prettiest gal in the whole country? Now, get your gear and I'll show you where you bunk. Got a room all fixed up and waiting for you inside. Then you got to eat." He half turned, shouted through the doorway. "Rosa! Got us a hungry man out here! Fix him up a big plate of vittles!"

After the huge meal of fried steak, potatoes, hot biscuits with fresh butter and wild honey, accompanied by strong, black coffee was over and Arlie's multitude of rapid-fire questions concerning the elapsed five years had been answered, they returned to the yard.

"Figured I'd show you around the place, kid," Arlie said as they stopped at the hitching rail. "Angelina would come, too, only she's taking a mite of rest. She just got in a couple hours before you. Been visiting with her folks over across the line in Paso Largo. You been there?"

Strike nodded. "Rode over last night. Ate there."

"Some town, eh? Wild as a ticked longhorn. You sleep there?"

Strike shook his head. "Stayed at the hotel in Long Pass. Don't think a man could get much sleep on the Mexican side of the border."

"For a fact. I'll have the hostler take care of your horse. Mighty nice-looking bay. Got me a sorrel that sure is a dandy. Figured we ought to get us a line of horses started, too."

They started for the barn with the gelding. Arlie said, "What'd you think of my wife?"

"Beautiful woman," Strike replied.

"She's Spanish. One of the genuine old aristocrats. Can trace her family right back to Spain. Was a time when they ran this country around here like kings and queens. Had a big ranch with all kinds of *peons,* all over the place. Reckon it was just like some of those big plantations we saw in the South that the war busted up."

Jim Strike was only half listening. He was

remembering the coldness in Angelina's eyes, the guarded restraint that definitely conveyed her resentment of him. As to why, he had not the remotest idea unless it was natural for a wife to be suspicious of her husband's partner. Perhaps, in time, he could overcome that. After they became better acquainted, maybe she would change. One thing that had puzzled him had been cleared up. Angelina was Spanish. He realized at the start she was not Mexican, being fair of skin and blonde. But he had not thought her an American, either.

"How did you meet your wife?" he asked.

"Met her when I was tracking down the owners of this land. It was an old Spanish land grant. Found out it belonged to the Mondragon's. That's the name of Angelina's people. Kid, there's over forty thousand acres of the best grazing land you ever rode across here in the valley. And another forty-five thousand on the flats around it. We got us a ranch of better'n eighty-five thousand acres and you won't find a better one, anywhere!"

They reached the barn. Two men came from the wide doorway — a short, squat Mexican and a tall, thin, older fellow, undoubtedly a Spaniard. Arlie handed the reins to the Mexican.

24

"This here is Manuel. Looks after the horses," Arlie explained. "And the other one is Francisco Vaca. He's sort of an overseer, only we ain't got much for him to be overseeing, yet. Reckon his family has been with the Mondragon's ever since they came into this country."

Strike shook hands first with Manuel, who bowed and showed his broad teeth in a wide grin, and then with Vaca. The Spaniard was somewhat more reserved with a certain haughtiness in his bearing. He held Strike's fingers only briefly and then turned to Silvershell.

"The *señora,* she is well?"

Arlie said, "Fine, fine. Little tired, that's all."

Vaca inclined his head politely and wheeled about. He waited while the hostler led the bay horse through the doorway and then followed him.

"Quite a people," Arlie said, shaking his head. "Don't reckon anything counts with them except Angelina. Everything else can go to grass so long as she's all right."

"You said something about her folks living across the border in Paso Largo. Why is it they aren't here, if this was their land?"

"Angelina's ma and pa never did live on it. Neither did their folks or the ones that came before them. Ain't been nothing on this ground until I came along and built the buildings."

They turned, started back toward the house. Strike said, "You get along with her people all right?"

Arlie shook his head ruefully. "I ain't so welcome with them. Any of them. They figured she married beneath herself, so to keep the peace we don't meet up any. Fact is, feeling is a little hard against me in the town, itself. When I got business dealings to be done, I go to Long Pass or maybe all the way to Mesilla. If it's something that has to be done on the Mexican side of the border, I let my wife handle it."

Strike nodded his understanding. The two towns were only five miles apart, Long Pass on the United States side of the line, Paso Largo on the Mexican.

"And talking about a wife," Silvershell continued, "about time you was thinking about getting one, ain't it? Mighty good feeling, having a woman all your own. Thought maybe you might have already got yourself hitched and, if so, I was planning to build another house, just like Angelina's and mine, for you. You ain't actually said, but are you married, yet?"

"Not me," Strike said at once.

"Any prospects?"

Strike shook his head. "Guess I haven't had time to do much looking around. Been on the move ever since we got out of the army."

"Well, could be you might get yourself one of those Shemonite gals from Long Pass. They come right pretty and got a lot of good horse-sense to go with it. Might have to sort of rustle you one, however. Shemonite people don't cotton much to their women marrying outside their own bunch. Reckon you noticed Long Pass was a Shemonite settlement."

Strike said, "I noticed. Main reason why I had to eat in Paso Largo. Everything but the hotel was closed up in Long Pass."

Silvershell cocked his head to one side, grinned as he looked closely at Strike. "You get in some kind of a ruckus in Largo last night? Appears to be a skinned place there on your jaw."

"Hold-up," Strike replied. "Five men jumped me just inside the valley."

Silvershell halted, his mouth dropping open in astonishment. "This morning? Here in the valley?"

Strike nodded. "Big man wearing Mexican clothes. A *vaquero*. Rest were Americans, I think. You ever hear of a man called Calloway and another known as Red? I heard those two names."

Arlie shook his head. "Plenty of *vaqueros* around, of course. And I don't recollect hearing the names you mention, either. They get anything?"

"Nothing. Didn't find my money on me. The part about it I don't understand is that they were looking for a thousand dollars they seemed to know I was carrying. You remember telling anybody about it?"

Again Silvershell displayed his amazement. "I never told anybody, excepting maybe Angelina! Fact is, I don't think you ever mentioned in your letter how much money you had. All there was about it was our agreement to each dig up a thousand. You sure they called the amount?"

"One thousand dollars. And this man Calloway said it looked like somebody got it wrong since they didn't find that much on me."

Silvershell wagged his head. "Beats all. Reckon maybe a dozen people knew you were coming in to join up with me but I can't figure who would know about the money. How did you manage to get away from them?"

"They just rode on, left me laying there in the road. Four of them went on back to

Paso Largo. The other, the *vaquero,* headed on into the valley."

"Never showed up around here," Arlie said. "I was out working around the corrals most of the morning. Never saw anybody until Angelina drove in with Tia Maria and Procopio."

"Who are they?"

"Couple of old Mexican folks. Sort of personal servants of Angelina. They been in the family for years, too, like Vaca and the others."

"Anywhere else he might be going? Somebody else have a place in the valley?"

"Nope," Arlie said promptly. "We're the only ones. No other houses around. Just ours. Of course, he might have swung east, cut back to Long Pass. Can't figure where else he would have gone. Mighty glad you didn't get hurt."

"Surprised me a little. Feel lucky they didn't put a bullet in my head."

"Quite a bit of that going on around here," Silvershell said then. "Hold-ups, I mean. Lot of hard cases hang around Paso Largo."

Strike nodded but a thought had just occurred to him. Thinking back it seemed to him that the *vaquero* didn't want him dead; that he left him alive intentionally. It didn't

29

make much sense, but it struck him as true.

They strolled slowly on, reached the last of the buildings before the valley closed sharply into the rugged canyon. A rail fence lay across the ravine's entrance, barring further progress.

"Bad, up there," Arlie explained, seeing the questioning look in Strike's eyes. "That's where the valley got its name — Tenkiller. Been several big landslides in there. About fifty years ago it came down good. Caught ten of Angelina's people and buried them before they could get out. The old *hacienda* was built in the canyon, about where the spring is, I reckon. Must be a hundred feet of rock and stuff on top of it."

"Ever come down again?"

"Sure. We have a wet spring, like we've just had, and shale starts coming down like all get out. Last year I lost a couple of horses in there. That's when I decided to put up this fence, so's the stock wouldn't wander in and get caught. One of these days I look for the whole kit and kaboodle to come piling down."

"Tenkiller Valley," Strike mused. "Wondered how it got that name."

"Probably a lot more than ten people buried in there. Stock, too, I'd bet. But there won't be no more of ours. Can't afford to lose any, not even one head."

They came about and walked back toward the ranch house. They stopped to admire Arlie's favorite horse, a huge, long-legged sorrel stallion that stood a full seventeen-hands high.

"Figure to use him for stud," Arlie explained when they again were moving on. "Build up a mighty fine strain of horses all our own. No sense in just thinking about cows."

Silvershell paused in stride, looked closely at Strike. "You ain't saying much, kid. Something on your mind? You don't like the place?"

Strike grinned, shook his head. "Guess I'm a bit snowed under by it all. Didn't expect you to have so much done, either, and it's a little hard to believe it's all ours."

"Well, it sure is!" Arlie declared, his huge, booming laugh echoing about the yard. "Course, there ain't much ranching being done right now on it. Took most of my thousand dollars to get hold of the land and build the buildings and such. But I did manage to latch on to about a hundred steers."

"Good start," Strike said. "Now we can take my thousand and buy more. Market is paying fifteen dollars a head right now for

31

beef. It will be even better this time next year when we're ready to sell."

"You got a full thousand dollars, then?"

Strike said, "Sure. Wouldn't be here if I didn't."

"No, reckon not. Should have known better than to ask. You always was a persnickety cuss for doing things up just so-so. Which sure is fine. Sooner we get started at this thing, the better. Soon as Angelina wakes up, we'll put our heads together and work out the details."

Angelina! Angelina!

The name flogged at Jim Strike's mind like a whip. Arlie could scarcely utter a complete sentence without mentioning her in some way. She was as much a part of the man as his right arm. That he worshipped her with a fanatic devotion was obvious.

And he reckoned it should be that way. When a man loved a woman, he should go all out for her. That would be the way of it with him, he supposed, if ever it came to pass. But he was not thinking about a wife in those moments; he was thinking of the ranch, of the partnership. He had an uneasy feeling that something was wrong, that all was not as it should be. He could almost feel the tension in the still air.

They reached the main house and stepped

up onto the gallery. Immediately, the door opened and a bulky, dark-faced woman came out. She shook her head at Silvershell, halting him in stride.

"The *señora* still sleeps," she stated flatly. "She is very tired."

Arlie stared at the woman for a moment. Then, "All right, Tia Maria." He turned and moved back off the porch. He grinned at Strike. "Guess we'll have to hold up on our little pow-wow for a spell, Jim. Maybe around dark."

Strike said, "Sure. No hurry. Think I'll saddle up and look around a bit."

"Fine. Got a few chores I ought to be doing, anyway. You take a run up on the flats. What stock we got is on the west side. See what you think of them. Then mosey on back about dark. Angelina will be awake by then."

Strike said, "Good. See you then," and wheeled for the barn.

CHAPTER THREE

In consideration for the bay gelding that had been traveling steadily for weeks, Strike selected another horse from the corral, a black with blazed face. He stood by while the hostler saddled and bridled him and Francisco Vaca watched with cool indifference, and then he rode from the yard. He kept to the west slope of the valley, following, more or less subconsciously, Arlie's suggestion to look over the jag of steers they owned as a starting herd.

Adding to the stock should not be too difficult. Cattle could be bought cheaply in Mexico, he had heard, and with the thousand dollars he had, they doubtless could procure a fair bunch of cattle across the border. And there were still plenty of wild, unmarked beef running loose in the brakes and hills. Round them up, wield the knife and iron, put them on good pasture for a year and they, too, would bring good market prices. He had heard it said that you could not make beef from a maverick but he had a hunch that any steer, put on plentiful grazing and good water, would have a change of nature.

He came to a trail that swung off to his right, into a long slash in the side of the valley. It was steep but safe, if taken slowly. He turned the black and began to climb toward the flat *mesa* above. When they came out on the top, Strike reined the horsed in, again struck by the lush magnificence of the country.

Mile upon mile, stretching out to infinity in gently rolling plains, all solidly covered with the gray-green of sweet grass — a cattleman's heaven. And half of it belonged to him. It was hard to believe that after all those years of hoping and working, it had finally come to be. But there it was, lying before him, all around him; what could be the finest cattle ranch in the West.

He glanced back down the trail he had just covered, thinking he heard sounds of an approaching horse. But seeing no one, he resumed his contemplation of the country. His eyes swept the horizon in search of the herd, but he saw only the endless world of grass. Assuming the stock was somewhere ahead, hidden from him by one of the innumerable low hillocks, he rode on. He had no definite plans in mind, no exact purpose; he simply needed to be alone, to ride and drink in the great beauty of the land.

A few minutes later, he heard a horse again and realized he was being followed. He felt edgy, recalling the hold-up and the subsequent beating he had taken, and a slow anger began to rise within him. He glanced about for places to conceal himself but the country offered few. It was mostly a land of rises and swales with only a few clumps of mesquite to be seen. Whoever it was on his trail was managing to keep from view by riding the hollows.

Two could play at that game, Strike decided and immediately swung the black down into a long, narrow depression. He walked the horse swiftly to the far end, broke over a small rise and dropped into another similar hollow. Tracing out its length he was able to double back and approach the trail he had followed at a different angle. He reached that point, halted. He was sitting quietly on the black when the rider suddenly appeared. It was Francisco Vaca.

Strike allowed him to draw near, until he was directly opposite, and then rode in on him suddenly. Vaca pulled in sharply, surprise tightening his thin, aquiline features.

"Don't like a man riding my trail," Strike said coldly. "Makes me a little jumpy sometimes."

Vaca removed his hat, shrugged. The man's hair, Strike noticed, was still jet black except along the temples where it was streaked with silver. He was older than he had appeared at the first meeting. "I am sorry, *señor*," he said, making no denial.

"You've caught up with me, now what do you want? What's it all about?"

Vaca replaced his hat, thought for a moment. Then, "It is nothing. You will forgive me, *señor*."

He wheeled his horse about, starting to retrace his steps. Strike's hand dropped to the pistol at his hip, anger lifting quickly within him. Vaca glanced back, smiled.

"Believe me, it is nothing."

Strike drew his gun. The Mexican had something on his mind and was on the verge of voicing it. Then he had changed his intention.

Strike said, "A man follows me for three miles. I want to know why." He brought the hammer of his weapon back, the click loud in the hot silence.

Vaca shook his head. "Another time, my friend," he said and rode on, turning his back to Strike.

Jim holstered his gun, watched him move off down the trail. He knew Strike would not shoot him in the back and evidently was gambling that the matter was not sufficiently serious to bring about a physical encounter. And he was right. Jim Strike watched him ride to the crest of a low ridge, drop down and out of sight. He sat for several minutes after the Mexican had gone, wondering at what the man had meant to do, or say. He shook his head. There was no way of knowing but it did further his conviction that something was wrong at the ranch.

He never found the herd. Possibly because his interest and thoughts had been diverted by the appearance of Francisco Vaca, or perhaps it was because he did not search too diligently. At any rate, he turned back some time later and, just before dark, rode into the hardpacked yard of the ranch.

He found Arlie and Angelina sitting in the shade of the front porch. Angelina had put on some sort of dressing gown, white and soft, that did little to conceal the shape of her body. Her hair, honey and gold in the afternoon light, was gathered loosely about her neck. She smiled as Strike stepped into the gallery.

Arlie greeted him with a shout. "Figured

it was about time for you to show, kid! Ready to get down to business?"

Strike nodded. "Whenever you are."

Arlie kicked a cane-bottomed chair toward him. "You see the herd? Not much to begin with, eh? But we'll build it up mighty fast, once we get going. How'd the range look to you? Real pretty, eh?"

Strike settled into the chair, considered the barrage of questions. "Didn't see the herd. Far as the range is concerned, never saw anything better, or as good. Won't take long to fatten beef on that grass."

"Right. And the sooner we get a herd bought and on it, the quicker they'll start putting on tallow. Angelina and me were just talking about it."

Strike looked closely at Arlie's wife, searching for some indication of her feelings toward him. Her lips were set in a faint smile and her eyes, deep green in the shadows, revealed nothing. He said, "What's the plan?"

"Just this, kid. Angelina and me will take your thousand cash and start out in the morning. We'll cross over the border and hit all the ranches along the way. I take Angelina because she knows all these people and can deal with them. Man and boy — how she can deal with them! She drives a fierce bargain, that woman! We'll keep on the move, buying up stock as we go, as long as the money holds out."

Arlie paused. He lit a thick, black cigar. He offered one to Strike who shook his head and reached for the sack of tobacco and papers in his pocket.

"Now, that beef likely won't look like much when you first see them. Mostly legs and horns strung together by hide. But give them a year on our range and I'll guarantee they'll bring top prices at any man's market. Agree?"

Strike said, "Sounds right to me."

"Don't know how much of a herd we can put together with a thousand dollars. That's all we got to buy with, your thousand. Like I told you, kid, used up most of mine getting the land and putting up these buildings and corrals. And, of course, we all got to eat. There's store grub that has to be bought and wages to pay. Guess maybe we got three hundred dollars or so left but we better hang onto that.

"But you can figure on us doing right well. Angelina will come out better than you and me could ever think of doing, I'll promise you that! Seems like those Mexicans and some of the *Americanos* over there just hone to sell her their stock — almost ready to give it to her, in fact."

Strike said, "That's the kind of buying we need done around here at the start. What about a crew?"

"That's where you come in. We got just five hands now, counting the hostler. They got to keep tabs on the ranch and the herd we're running, while we're gone. Thing for you to do is to ride in and recruit us a crew. Many as you think we'll need."

"That will depend on how much stock you're able to buy."

"Better plan on four, maybe five drovers. Make it easier to trail a herd without danger of loss. Some of the men we might keep on permanent, others we can turn loose when the drive is finished."

Strike nodded. "When will I pick up the herd and where?"

"Let's see, this is Sunday. Minute we make a deal, we'll have the rancher cut out our stock and move them to Galesburg. Little town on the border, about two days or so southwest of here. We'll gather there. I'd say you ought to be able to move the herd out on Friday."

Angelina, silent through it all, spoke up. "You won't find much in Long Pass, Jim. Most likely you'll have to cross over to Paso Largo to find riders. Usually quite a few

41

around there, looking for work."

Strike said, "Thanks, I'll remember that." He was looking closely at Angelina.

She laughed. "You are surprised to hear me speak English so well? I learned at a convent."

"Speaks it better'n me," Arlie declared. "Well, I guess we're all set, kid. Except for one more thing. I got some papers made up showing we're partners in this *fandango*. Maybe they ain't the legalest things you ever saw but they'd stand up in court if ever they had to. I've already signed them. Now, all you have to do is put your John-Henry on the line and that part will be taken care of."

Jim accepted the papers, slid a glance at Angelina. She was looking down, her face hidden from him. He read the simple agreement, affixed his signature, and handed the sheet back to Silvershell. Then he rose, went to the bedroom assigned him earlier in the day and procured the necessary thousand dollars. When he returned, he handed it to Arlie.

The big man grinned, ran his broad hand through his hair. "We're in business, partner!" he boomed. "And I'm dang sure none of us is ever going to regret it. Give us a couple, three good years and we'll be rich!"

Jim shook Arlie's hand and looked beyond

42

the Missourian to the girl. She was watching them now, her cameo-clean face stilled, her lips set, eyes inscrutable.

"What do you say to a little game of penny-ante? Just to pass the time away. But I warn you, kid, this woman of mine is no greenhorn at cards! She'll clean your plow, you ain't careful!"

It was near midnight when Angelina pulled a robe over her slender figure and slipped quietly from the bedroom where Arlie lay snoring deeply. She made her way softly to the rear of the house where Tia Maria and Procopio maintained quarters. Arlie and Jim Strike had stayed up much longer than she had expected, talking over the days when they were in the army and relating their subsequent experiences after they were out.

She had managed to get the note written to Pen Moraga while they were reminiscing, telling him that she and Arlie would soon visit him for the purpose of buying stock, and that, during the time they were there, it was an absolute necessity that she see him alone. Since Pen had failed in their plan to hold up and rob Jim Strike of his thousand dollars, something else had to be done. The partnership of Strike and her husband had already advanced much further than she wished. The note should have been sent earlier, but that had been impossible. Now old Procopio would be pressed to get it delivered in time.

She had some difficulty in arousing the man. Finally he came to the door, wearing only his underclothes and his shapeless cotton trousers.

"Qué pasa, señora?"

She handed him the letter. "Take this to Moraga at once. He is at his ranch."

The ancient *peon*'s wrinkled face drew into a dark frown. "But, *señora,* it is a far ride and I have done much today. I am tired —"

"It must be taken now," Angelina said sharply. "If you are no longer able to serve me when I have need, then I shall have to get someone else. A younger man who will not complain."

Procopio's thin shoulders sagged. "I shall go, *señora,* never fear. It shall be as you wish."

"You will leave immediately?"

Procopio nodded. "At once, *señora.*"

"No one is to see you leave, old one. And you are not to say where you have been when you return. Is that well understood?"

Procopio nodded. "It is understood." He looked down at the folded, sealed envelope in his clawlike hand. "It is of much importance, this letter?"

Angelina said, "Very important. It has much to do with the *Hacienda de Mondragon.* Your haste in getting it to my cousin will speed the day when this country again will be the home of all our people."

Pen Moraga was not, in actuality, her cousin. He was no relation at all, but it pleased Angelina to have others think so. It explained the many times they had been seen together, by night in Paso Largo and on the *mesas* in the day. Of course Procopio and Francisco Vaca and the others of the family knew better, but they would say nothing. They thought only of the day when her promise to them became fulfilled and the old Spanish *hacienda* of the Mondragon's once again lived and flourished as in the old days.

And Arlie believed they were cousins. That was most important, for without him she could never have rebuilt the *rancho.* And without him there would have been no Jim Strike and his thousand American dollars which she would now use to stock the range with cattle.

Old Procopio's head had come up at her words. "It is good. It is fitting that it should be I who carries a letter of such importance." He bowed slightly. "I go now, *señora*."

Angelina walked back to the kitchen where, from a window, she could observe the barn. She waited until the old man had entered the darkened structure and, after a few minutes, returned to the yard. He was leading the small, gray pony he called his own. A long, hard journey was ahead of Procopio, but she could depend on him to make it.

She watched him climb stiffly onto his heavy Mexican saddle and walk the gray quietly out of the yard. He kept to the corrals until he was well beyond the buildings and soon was out of sight. She turned, then, and walked slowly back toward her bedroom, halting just outside the door. The proof that Arlie slept soundly was evident. She looked toward Jim Strike's room thoughtfully, but rejected the idea that had entered her mind. Jim Strike was not the sort who could be swayed by a woman's charms. He was not like Pen Moraga or Chris Calloway or Bill Trenchard or any of the others she had used. And he was not like Arlie Silvershell. She had a disturbing intuition that his steady gray eyes saw deep into her and recognized many things she did not wish him or anyone else to know.

And because of that he posed great danger for her and her plans. Therefore he must be removed before he could do harm.

CHAPTER FOUR

Angelina and Arlie left shortly after seven o'clock the next morning. They were driving a span of blacks, not fast animals but tough, and they rode in the yellow-wheeled buggy. They carried no food or provisions other than a canteen of water, for the hospitality of the land was such that they could expect to dine with ranchers along their route whenever the proper hour for meals overtook them.

Jim Strike stood on the gallery of the ranch house and watched them ride out of the yard. A few minutes before the departure, while Arlie was yet inside, he had strolled up alongside the vehicle where Angelina, chic and practical in trim corduroy, black patent-leather boots and a wide-brimmed, low-crowned hat, sat on the cushioned seat. She regarded him with that cool, impersonal surveillance of hers.

He said, "Hope you have good luck. And

don't be too fussy about the steers. We can soon fatten them up."

She started to make some quick reply, thought better of it. She looked away, her eyes reaching out across the wide, green prairies. "It is a wonderful land, isn't it?" she remarked, her voice almost dreamy.

"Finest I've ever laid eyes on," Strike answered. "One thing more. Haven't had a chance to say this yet, but Arlie's my best friend. Like for it to be that way with us, too."

Angelina did not turn her face to him. She said, "Of course," and let it drop there.

At that moment Silvershell came through the doorway. He was like a small child, happy and overflowing with joy. The prospect of Angelina and himself making a trip of several days duration, of being constantly together, delighted him. He slapped Strike on the shoulder and climbed into the carriage, grinning broadly.

"Be seeing you, pard!" he yelled and swung the vehicle out of the yard.

Strike watched them pull away, pleased with Arlie's happiness. A lonely man himself, often longing for the love and tender affections of a woman, a wife, he could easily imagine the joy in Arlie's heart. He wished only that he could remove the doubt

49

and suspicions, or whatever it was, that Angelina held for him.

He was in no great hurry to reach Long Pass or its noisy echo across the border in Mexico. He spent most of the morning making repairs on his gear and seeing to a shoe that had come loose on the gelding. There was also the matter of arranging for extra horses and a chuck wagon to be awaiting him at Galesburg on Friday when the trail drive would begin. Francisco Vaca was not round the ranch but with the help of Tia Maria and the cook, Rosa, he managed to make the hostler understand his wishes.

He rode from the ranch near noon, taking it easy, and arrived in Long Pass after sundown. The clerk at the hotel who recognized him from the first time, gave him the same room. He did his own stabling chores for the bay and was in bed an hour later. He was in need of sleep. Arlie Silvershell liked to stay up late.

Long Pass appeared somewhat different in daylight. The next morning, as he walked along the street in search of a café, he was impressed by the air of activity. There were several wagons and buckboards drawn up to the numerous hitching rails and not a few buggies and fringed surries. Most of the persons he saw were Shemonites, dressed in their usual garb of black worsted trousers, black sateen shirts and round, low-crowned hats. The town's main industry seemed to be feed and seed supply with the usual general-merchandise store to furnish clothing, household wares and such.

As he had discovered on his previous visit, there were no saloons, no gambling palaces, no houses with curtained windows where the company of girls might be purchased. It was a sober, friendly place with most of those he passed on the boardwalks nodding and according him a welcoming smile. Arlie had been right about the Shemonite women, too. They were good to look at, well formed and usually pretty despite the drabness of their Mother Hubbard costumes.

He located the restaurant near the end of the street. It was a combination bakery and café, doing business in a room hardly larger than his quarters in the hotel. There were three tables with four chairs each, placed about on a cleanly swept floor. He sat down at one. A heavy curtain, hanging from a doorway which led into an adjoining room, parted as he settled himself. A tall, brown-haired girl with deep blue eyes entered. Jim half rose from his chair.

The girl smiled at his courtesy. "Thank you. Please sit down."

She cocked her head slightly, setting a pretty pose. "What will you have?"

He found his voice. "Breakfast. Whatever you have that's ready."

"Fried eggs, potatoes, fresh bacon. Doughnuts if you like and hot biscuits. Will that do?"

"Do fine. Like some coffee."

The girl smiled again. "Of course. I'll bring it right away."

She turned about, slender and willowy in her fitted white dress. She was back in only moments, bringing him a large cup of steaming, dark brew.

"Just what I need," Strike murmured as she placed it before him. He felt a sudden and unaccountable need to talk more with her, an unusual and hard-to-understand symptom in him. Ordinarily, he had small time for women, scarcely giving them a second glance unless it was for obvious physical reasons. Somehow this tall girl with the serene, blue eyes and calm features affected him differently. She had seized his attention and was holding it by the solitary power of her personality and deep, natural beauty.

"Aren't you —," he began, hesitantly, treading on the unfamiliar ground of striking up a conversation with a strange lady —

"one of the Shemonite people? You don't wear black like the others."

She glanced down at the front of her garment, brushed an imaginary speck from its spotless surface. "Oh, yes, but being the town's baker and restaurant owner, I am accorded some leniency — as long as I do not appear on the street. It seems traditional that bakers wear white. I've never known if it is to keep the spilled flour from showing or to point up the cleanliness, or lack of it, to the customers." She laughed again, the light-hearted tinkling of it filling the small room.

"It becomes you," Strike said and was immediately awed and surprised that the words came so easily from his throat. "You lived here long?"

"Five years this spring, I came here with my husband."

Apparently she saw some break in his expression for she added, "My husband was killed, drowned in a flash flood soon after we arrived. I had no other place to go so I just stayed on and eventually opened my shop."

"Nice town," Strike offered, relief plain in his voice. "Nice and quiet, anyway."

"You're a stranger here, aren't you?"

He said, "Yes. Rode in a couple of days

53

ago. I'm in partners with a friend of mine on a ranch, half a day or so west of here. Maybe you know him. Arlie Silvershell."

She thought for a moment, pressing her hands together before her as she looked out into the street, her profile soft and lovely. She shook her head. "No, I don't believe I've heard of him. Not many travelers stop here. Most go on across the border. I have been wondering why you didn't."

"Here to hire on a crew of drovers," he said at once. "Name is Strike. Jim Strike."

"I'm Hannah Moore," she said and extended her hand.

He shook it gravely, noting her long fingers, cool and strong and well-cared for. He continued to hold her hand, unaware of the passing seconds. She carefully withdrew it. He looked up quickly to find her studying him with a curious, somewhat puzzled look, her head again tipped slightly in that fetching way of hers.

"Sorry," he murmured. "Reckon I wasn't thinking."

She said, "Of course. Now, about drovers. I'm afraid you won't find any around here. Most likely you will have to cross over the border and try the town on the Mexican side. Cowboys don't hang around Long Pass once they learn there are no attractions here."

Strike said, "Depends on what you consider an attraction," and was again startled by his own boldness.

Hannah Moore regarded him calmly, her smile sweet. "Why, Mr. Strike, I like that! I believe you really meant that as a compliment."

He said, "It was. And call me Jim."

"Well, then, Jim, thank you. And if you will call me Hannah we'll be on even footing. Now, I had better get to your breakfast or it will be dinner time."

Strike picked up his cup, followed her through the curtained doorway. "Mind if I watch?"

She turned about and gave him a serious, level look, as if assessing him thoroughly. She smiled. "Of course not. You are welcome to sit in my kitchen if you wish."

"When a man's going to be a steady customer," Strike remarked, walking farther into the room, "I guess he has a right to see where what he eats comes from."

She had halted before a narrow table placed against the opposite wall. A row of variously sized pots and pans hung above it. From a shelf she took a side of bacon wrapped in muslin, removed the cloth and with a curved knife carved off several slices.

This done, she paused and glanced over her shoulder at him.

"Steady customer?" she repeated, her brows lifting.

Jim Strike grinned. "The steadiest you'll ever have," he said.

Chapter Five

Hannah Moore and Angelina were both right. An hour's search about Long Pass failed to produce a single rider interested in a job. So late in the morning, he rode over the line into Mexico and traveled the short distance to Paso Largo.

The town dozed in the steadily rising heat. Children played in the dust along the roadside, a few alcohol-logged cowboys lay where they had collapsed near the saloon, and gaunt dogs had already found shady spots beneath wagons and behind buildings, all of which appeared weather-worn and shabby in daylight's harsh reality.

Under the kindly disguise of darkness and mellow lamplight, the town had looked quite different to Jim Strike during his first visit. Now, Paso Largo presented itself as it truly was: a collection of old, run-down, wood and *adobe* shacks and buildings standing drunkenly along rubbish-strewn streets. But that didn't affect business. Horses stood in considerable numbers at the hitch rails along the dusty street.

He selected the largest of the saloons, The *Toro-Rojo,* the Red Bull, and slanted the bay toward it. He dismounted, tied the gelding, entered the building and walked to the bar. He ordered a beer from the frozen faced bartender, an American, and then turned and glanced over the patrons. There were a dozen or so men in the place, two or three pretty, smiling Mexican girls. He waited a minute until they had all made their close and wary inspection of him and then spoke.

"Name is Strike. I'm needing a crew for a trail drive. That done, there'll likely be a few permanent jobs for those who want them. Anybody here interested?"

There was a long pause. Finally, one man, a sun-blackened oldster with a long scar tracing across the left side of his face, asked, "How long's this here drive goin' to last?"

"Week, maybe a little more. Moving a herd from a place called Galesburg to a ranch in Tenkiller Valley."

From behind him Strike heard the bartender grunt in surprise. "You say Tenkiller? That's hoodoo country."

There was a long minute of quiet. "Whose ranch? Your'n?" another cowboy asked.

"Mine and my partner's. Name of Silver-shell."

"Never heard of him," the man replied and lapsed back into his chair.

The scar-faced rider spoke up. "Well, I'm down here just waitin' for another drive to line out. Reckon I could use a bit of extra money. What's the pay, mister?"

"Dollar a day and keep for the drive. Any man who decides to stay on permanent, once we get the herd moved, we'll pay thirty dollars a month and keep."

The scar-faced man said, "Well, beats buckin' a faro table. When you figure to pull out, Mr. Strike?"

"Tomorrow morning, daybreak. Meet me across the line at the hotel." Strike pulled a sheet of paper and a pencil from his pocket. "What's your name?"

"Aaron Hendrix."

Strike wrote it down. He glanced up. "Anybody else?"

A gangling youngster got to his feet, lifted his hand. "Count me in, Mr. Strike."

Jim looked the boy over. He was young, too young in years to have much experience. But it began to appear he could not be choosey. "All right. Name?"

"Oren Smith."

A tall, thin cowboy with a straggling, long

mustache leaned forward in his chair. "What you say about that bein' hoodoo country, Charlie?"

The bartender said, "Been some bad things happen around there. People droppin' out of sight. Landslides and the like."

"In the end of the canyon," Strike said. "But that was a long time ago and anyway, you don't go near the canyon if you don't want to. You'll be working range in the opposite direction."

The cowboy with the mustache drummed on the table with his finger tips. "Sure don't hanker to tangle with a jinx, but I could use that money." He stopped, glanced at the man next to him. "How about you, Carl? You willin'?"

"If you are."

"Reckon you can count us in then, Mr. Strike. I'm Pete Longbridge. My partner here is Carl Thomas."

Strike added their names to the list. Including himself he now had a crew of five. Enough, possibly, for the size herd Arlie and Angelina would be able to buy with the amount of cash they had to spend. But he wanted to take no chances. Better to use up a few extra dollars and safeguard the herd's delivery than lose it all because of a false sense of economy.

He said, "Can use a couple more. Anybody else interested?"

There was no response. Strike folded the sheet of paper and thrust it into his shirt pocket. "All right. You men who signed up, meet me in Long Pass, like I said. Bring your own horse and gear. I'll stand you to breakfast. Then we'll pull out."

"How about spare horses?" Longbridge asked. "We goin' to have a *remuda?*"

"Be horses waiting at Galesburg for us. Along with a chuck wagon."

Young Oren Smith said, "Know a couple of more boys who might be willin' to sign on. You want I should tell them about it?"

"Sure. They can find me around the hotel in Long Pass rest of the day. Or bring them along in the morning. Now, you all belly-up to the bar and have a drink on me," he added, and laid a gold coin on the counter. "I'll see you in the morning."

There was a general move towards the bar and Strike started for the swinging doors. Halfway across the room, Aaron Hendrix intercepted him.

"Mr. Strike, just been thinkin' about your sayin' they was to be some steady jobs on that ranch of yours. I'm gettin' a mite old for drovin', seein's how I won't see this side of forty-five again and besides, I got a family I sure ought to be lookin' after. Wife and a couple of boys. That offer you made include them, too?"

Jim said, "Sure. Might have to throw a house together for you to live in, but we can manage that."

"Then I reckon I'm one of your regular hands from now on, Mr. Strike, you bein' willin'."

"I'm willing. And it would be a little easier if you'd call me Jim. That's my name."

Aaron Hendrix scratched at his gray-stubbled chin. "Well, I don't know about that. Always called the boss man, mister. It bein' all the same to you, I reckon I'd just like to keep on doin' it."

Strike grinned. "Whatever you say, Aaron." He ducked his head at the old rider and started again for the doors.

Hendrix halted him once more. "Got one more favor I'd sure like to ask, Mr. Strike. My woman and the boys is stayin' over with friends in Mesilla, waitin' on me. Now that I'm goin' to be set, permanent-like, ought to get them to comin' this way. Trouble is I never did learn to do any readin' or writin'. I was wonderin' if you'd pen me a letter, tellin' her to pack up and come on? Sure would take it as a mighty big favor."

Strike said, "Sure. Be glad to."

Hendrix got an envelope and a clean sheet of paper from the bartender. Sitting down at one of the tables, Strike wrote the message for the cowboy, directing his wife to quarter at the hotel in Long Pass when she arrived and to wait for her husband there. She and the two boys could take their meals at Hannah Moore's. He would set it up with the clerk and Hannah, he assured Hendrix. When it was done, he sealed the envelope and handed it to Hendrix. Together they passed through the doorway onto the porch, Strike to obtain supplies for their coming ride to Galesburg, Hendrix to get his letter enroute.

Halfway across the gallery, Strike came to an abrupt stop. Two riders coming down the street had caught his eye. A tall blond cowboy and a redhead. Calloway and his friend of the hold-up incident. They angled for the saloon. Anger rose quickly within Jim Strike as the memory of those brutal moments on the road crowded through his mind. He stepped from the porch into the loose dust of the street, his face hard and still.

Beside him Aaron Hendrix said, "What's the trouble, Mr. Strike? What's up?"

Strike said, "Watch the redhead for me."

He stopped near the rack and waited while

63

Calloway and the redhead swung in. Calloway saw him then. He hauled up short and sat quietly in his saddle, making no move to dismount. He recognized Strike with a faint, curling sneer on his long lips.

"Get down off that horse," Strike commanded in a cold voice.

Calloway made no move to comply. He glanced sidewards to Red. "Looky who's here!"

"Get down," Strike repeated softly.

Calloway only stared at him. A sudden wave of anger boiled up and brimmed over inside Strike. He took a long, rushing step forward. He reached out, grabbed the cowboy's arm and pulled. Calloway came piling out of the saddle and crashed to the ground. Red muttered something and leaped from his horse.

Aaron Hendrix's drawling voice halted him. "Now, hold on right there, redhead. Don't say as I rightly know what's goin' on here but I reckon it's atwixt them two. You just come back up here on the gallery and let them settle it themselves."

Calloway lifted himself from the dust, his face scarlet with fury, curses rumbling from his lips. Men were coming from all nearby buildings at a noisy run. A crowd quickly began to gather. Strike moved out into the

64

center of the street, away from the horses and the rack and the edge of the porch. He watched the husky Calloway through narrowed eyes.

Calloway lunged. Strike took a swift sidestep. As the blond cowboy went by, he drove his balled fist into the side of the man's head. The power of the down-sledging blow and the cowboy's own impetus sent him stumbling on. He tripped and fell, face down, but he was back on his feet in a wink and again charged Strike.

He was not to be caught a second time. He slowed his wild rush as he drew close. He dropped into a crouch, began to weave back and forth, his fists upraised and before him. Strike watched him closely. Calloway had much to learn about fighting. Strike allowed the man to move in, start a swing. With the speed of a gunflash, he lashed out. He knocked Calloway's faint guard aside with a sweeping left and drove his knotted right fist into the cowboy's unprotected jaw. Calloway went back to his heels. His arms flung outward, as though released by hidden springs. He went over, flat on his back.

The crowd milled about excitedly, shouting advice and encouragement. From the tail of his eye, Jim caught the glitter of sunlight on a lawman's badge. But the marshal or sheriff, whichever he was, remained where he stood and made no move to halt the fight. Strike kept his attention focused on Calloway. The cowboy was getting slowly to his feet, his eyes glazed.

"You had enough?" Strike snarled. "I hope not. Figure I still owe you a little more."

Calloway lunged at him, choosing to fight. He caught Strike with a straight left, followed by a right that stung surprisingly. A shout burst from the throats of those in the crowd who were Calloway partisans. Strike pivoted away. Calloway, now encouraged, bored in recklessly. Strike whirled unexpectedly and swung hard. He stopped the blond cowboy dead cold with a stiff drive to the belly. He turned him half about with a blow that landed high on the left breast. Calloway suddenly was gasping for breath. Strike staggered him with a solid smash to the jaw that was heard throughout the street. He drew back, prepared to follow up with another. He checked himself. Calloway's eyes were empty. His mouth sagged and his arms hung limp at his sides. To hit him again would be like hitting a dead man.

"All right, Calloway," he said, "we're quits."

He turned away, threw his hard glance to the gallery. The redhead had disappeared.

He was having none of it. Strike shrugged and walked toward the gelding. The crowd split to let him through, some congratulating him, others only staring at him silently. There was a surge as Calloway's friends moved in to where he stood in shocked defeat.

Aaron Hendrix came off the porch, his seamy, dark face wearing a wide, happy grin. "What was that there all about, Mr. Strike? Man, you sure did hand it to that feller!"

Strike yanked at the gelding's leathers and freed him from the rack. "Personal matter," he said. He was still taut, anger and excitement piling through his long body.

"Well, whatever for, that was a mighty good job you done on him! Got me a feelin' I'm goin' to plumb enjoy workin' for you!"

Strike barely heard the old puncher's remarks. He caught the glance of the tall lawman, waiting for him just ahead. He was an American, a deputy U.S. Marshal, according to the star on his vest. The man would have no authority in Mexico, of course, but it seemed he had something on his mind. Strike prodded the bay toward the disapproving shape of the lawman. The marshal reached out, hooked his fingers into the gelding's bridle, halted him.

A suppressed fury thudded through Strike's blood. "Something bothering you, Marshal?" he asked in a voice that trembled slightly.

The lawman said, "Always riles my guts to see troublemakers like you running loose! You damned Texas cowboys seem to think you own any town you happen to be riding through!"

"Wrong both times!" Strike snapped. "I'm no Texan and I'm no troublemaker. This thing got started a few days back. Was just finishing it up."

The deputy stared at him, plainly disbelieving. He shook his head. "Sure, sure. Well, I'll tell you this. It's a good thing it was one of your own kind you jumped. Had it been one of the Mexicans, I'd have been glad to help the *soldados* throw you in for a few months!"

Strike clung to his temper. He had arrived at the point where he would just as soon leave his saddle and take on the lawman, as he had Calloway. But the reasonableness of the man stayed the anger that pushed at him.

"You through, Marshal? Then let go my horse."

The lawman released his fingers, stepped back. "Ride on out of here before I change my mind," he said.

Strike favored him with a hard grin. "On my way," he said.

It likely did appear that he had walked up to Calloway and deliberately picked a quarrel. Probably everyone in Paso Largo, including the lawman, thought that was the way of it. He should set them straight, particularly the deputy marshal. Then he thought better of it, shrugged. It was pointless to explain anything. He touched the bay with his spurs and they moved off down the street, for Long Pass.

Chapter Six

He spent the balance of that day buying sufficient grub for the crew and himself to last
until they reached Galesburg. There, they
would pick up the wagon, delivered to that
point by the ranch hostler, along with the
extra horses that would be needed.

He was finished late in the afternoon and
spent the balance of the daylight hours with
Hannah Moore in her small restaurant,
drinking coffee, eating his evening meal and
talking. He enjoyed those restful minutes.
While he was with her some of the deep,
long-reaching loneliness seemed to slip from
his tall frame and he became a different
man, one who found words easily and spoke
them readily.

It was a new experience for Jim Strike.
Never before, with any man or woman, had
he felt such ease and contentment. And that
night after he had stretched out full length
on the artillery caisson hard bed of his hotel

room, he wondered about it. Hannah Moore affected him differently than any woman had ever done; perhaps it was because he had never before been interested in the opposite sex. He sat up suddenly, an extraordinary thought pushing into his mind.

Was he in love with Hannah?

Was that what this different feeling was all about? He guessed it was so, only he didn't have sense enough to realize it. He grinned into the darkness of the stuffy room. Maybe they would have to build that second ranch house Arlie had talked about sooner than they expected! Of course, he thought then, soberly, Hannah might have some other ideas. Such a fine woman was not likely to go jumping off into a matter as big as marriage without first taking a good, long look at it.

Except for the vague uneasiness created by Angelina's unfriendly attitude, the attempted hold-up and Francisco Vaca's trailing of him that first day, he could have been completely happy. Now, it all hung like a threatening shadow overhead, menacing his hopes and ambitions for the future.

The entire crew showed up that next morning, including one of the riders Oren Smith had mentioned. He was a little older than

Smith and his name was Davis. Strike added his name to his list and escorted them all to Hannah's where she served them a monstrous breakfast designed to last them out the full day. While they ate, Strike inspected their horses and gear. Satisfied, except for the lack of a canteen on the part of Davis, he returned to the inside.

He ate his own meal then, taking his time. When he was finished, the others were outside waiting for him. Davis had been sent to the nearest store to complete his outfit and he, too, was back and ready to ride, the canteen filled and hanging from his saddle. Strike paid his bill and moved to the front of the café. Hannah followed at his heels. When he halted at the door she laid a hand on his arm.

"How long will you be gone?"

He said, "Couple of weeks, more or less."

"I'll miss you," she murmured, her absolute honesty covering the boldness of her words. "Will there be any danger?"

He grinned. "Only from falling off my horse, and I haven't done that in quite a spell."

Her shoulders fell slightly, signifying her relief. "I shall be looking for you, Jim. Will you come as soon as the drive is finished?"

He grinned broadly again. "I'll be here,

looking for my breakfast two weeks from right now! Figure on it."

"I shall," she said. She moved up close to him. She reached up, took his face between her hands and pulled him down, kissing him lightly on the cheek.

For a moment he was startled, surprised. He stared at her, bewildered. The idea that she, too, might feel as he did had been too remote. He had planned upon a lengthy campaign for her favor, hoping to win her for his own, eventually. But now — he spun quickly. He took her by the shoulders, drew her hard against him. He lowered his head, kissed her firmly, almost brutally, on the lips.

He did not immediately release her but held her tightly for a long minute as though gathering and storing up the memory of what was happening to them. Then he stepped back.

"I'll be here, sooner than two weeks if I can manage it. We've got a lot of important talking to do about the future."

She smiled. "I'll be waiting, Jim. Good-by."

"So long," he said and opened the door and walked out into the street.

They rode out of Long Pass ten minutes later, Strike and Aaron Hendrix leading the crew which had paired up; Oren Smith with his friend Keno Davis, Longbridge with Carl Thomas. They maintained an easy but steady pace following the course of the sun and when darkness came they pulled in for a night camp on the edge of a wild and broken badlands. Longbridge, scouting about, located a small waterhole suitable for the horses and they spread their blanket rolls close by.

Squatting around the fire later, drinking the last of the coffee, Strike called for their attention. "Road we take skirts these brakes, according to the information I got. But we can cut straight across if we like."

"Be rough goin'," Carl Thomas commented.

Strike said, "Agreed. But we can take it slow. We don't pick up the herd until Friday, even Saturday if we need an extra day. What I'd like to do is work these brakes for stock. My partner and I are just building up a spread and we can use all the cows we can get our hands on."

"Heard tell there was a lot of unbranded stuff not belongin' to anybody, runnin' loose down there," Longbridge said.

"Right," Strike said, "and I'd sure like to have some of it. I realize beeves out of there wouldn't be worth much, now. They generally mean trouble. But a few of them we could handle easy enough. Put them on good grass and water for a year and they'll shape up fine. Time we get around to drive to market, they ought to be in good condition."

Aaron Hendrix wagged his head. "They'll be mighty ornery critters, wilder'n a turpentined cat. But I reckon it won't be too much of a chore, chousin' them out of there."

"I don't want anybody or any of the horses hurt. Understand that. Loose stock's not that important to me."

"How about the branded stuff, you want them, too?" Longbridge asked, looking intently at Strike.

Strike felt the eyes of all the riders upon him, waiting out his reply. He said, "No branded cattle. I don't want to see a mark anywhere on the stock we get out of the brakes."

Longbridge grunted, satisfied. "Just wanted to get it straight in my head," he said.

"Good. Now, turn in. We'll make an early start."

Later, while Strike was standing aside from the camp, on the lip of a butte which dropped off into the brakes country, Hendrix strolled up and hunkered down on his heels. He said nothing for several moments, spending much time twisting up a thin, brown cigarette, lighting it and tamping out the match in the coarse soil.

"Was just thinkin'," he said, finally, "about them mavericks down there in the brush."

"So?"

"Figure it would be a plumb good way for a man to size up his crew."

Strike grinned into the star-flecked darkness of the sky. He had not fooled the old cowboy for a moment. After a day's work in the rough country below, he would know well who the experienced hands among his riders were and how far he could trust each man's judgment.

"Good place to shake the kernels out of the husks."

"Something that had to be done," Strike said. "Herd means everything to my partner and me. We lose it, we can forget ever having a spread of our own. Man doesn't take chances at such times as this."

Hendrix nodded. "Reckon that's gospel but I don't figure you got much to worry about. Couple of our crew may be a mite wet behind the ears but they been around some. I reckon they can wrassle a steer along with most waddies. Ain't how old a man is that counts, it's what he's been doing with the years he's got."

And it proved out that Aaron Hendrix was right. Strike quickly saw that none of the five men was a greenhorn at handling cattle, although the difference between Hendrix and the others was marked. The old rider seemed to do twice the work with only half the effort the others, particularly Keno Davis and Young Oren Smith, expended. He was a natural hand with cattle and Strike was pleased he had signed him on as a permanent employee. He would make a good foreman. Strike made a mental note to talk it over with Arlie. On the whole he was well satisfied with them all. When they pulled up onto the flats near dark, they had accumulated a total of twenty-one steers, the self-appointed leader of which proved to be a belligerent, red-eyed, old black-and-white Mexican longhorn with a six-foot rack.

Longbridge was for putting a bullet between the eyes of the renegade immediately, predicting nothing but trouble from him, but Strike stayed his hand. A bull, such as the black-and-white, properly handled, was a great help when the herd was on the move. Other cattle follow such a leader blindly. The trick was to keep him headed right and Strike, after watching Aaron Hendrix work, knew he had a man who could control the big longhorn.

They traveled slowly the next day, taking their time, keeping the small jag of stock moving along in easy, orderly fashion. "Breaking them to trail," Aaron termed it. They kept wide of the badlands, not wanting the stock to try for a return visit. Close to sundown they topped a roll of low hills and were in sight of Galesburg — a store, four or five shacks and a broadly spreading waterhole.

"There she is!" Oren Smith sang out. "There's the town!"

"And I reckon there's your herd, Mr. Strike," Hendrix said and pointed with stubby finger to a dark blur off to the north of the sky-mirroring lake.

CHAPTER SEVEN

When they were no more than a few hundred yards from the herd, a rider separated from the others and rode toward them. He stopped on the breast of a knoll, his horse standing broadside to the light-flared horizon.

"Strike?" he called out as they drew nearer.

"Here," Jim said and pulled away from the others. He drifted the bay up to the man's side. "My name's Strike."

The man, a middle-aged, red-faced individual, stuck out his hand. "I'm Conover. Glad you showed up. Five hundred head in that herd down there and I got just three men to hold them. Been plumb jumpy. If they'd spooked, we'd sure been out of luck."

"Five hundred head!" Strike echoed. "You sure of that?" It was unbelievable that Arlie and Angelina could have done so well. An average of two dollars a steer!

"That's what you got. Your partner stayed around here until the last of them was drove in, yesterday. They been comin' all week, mostly. Biggest bunch from the Pitchfork outfit. Why? You not expectin' that big a herd? Looks like you got plenty of help."

Strike said, "Lucky there, too. Fact is, I didn't know what to expect. Stranger to this country and my partner and his wife did all the buying. Two dollars a head for cattle is about as low as I ever heard of paying."

Conover shrugged. "Depends on who's buying. Usual price for Mexican stuff runs three, maybe four dollars. What did you pay for that jag you drove in?"

"Nothing but a little work. Combed them out of the brakes on the way up. All maverick stuff."

Conover shook his head. "Man earns anything he digs out of that place. Except there's a young fortune hid in that brush, was a man to get after it right hard. You see much branded stock?"

"Few."

"Been thinkin' about takin' a couple of my boys and doin' a little hazin' in there myself. Now, seein' what you got, I reckon I sure will. Maybe before the summer's over. Only thing is, I got to find me the time. Always somethin' else that's got to be tended. You ready to take over your herd?"

Strike said, "Might as well. Let you get started on your way. You got the papers?"

Conover said, "No papers. Your partner took them with him. Don't reckon you'll be needin' them anyway."

Strike frowned. "Maybe not," he said, "but I always feel a little more comfortable with a bill of sale in my pocket. That hostler get here with my extra horses and the chuck wagon?"

"Wagon and about a dozen animals over there by the pond. Mexican man brought them, then lit right out for home."

Strike swore softly. Conover glanced at him.

"Was he supposed to be waitin'?"

Strike nodded. "I guess I didn't make him — or the woman that was doing my talking for me, understand. I figured to use him as trail cook."

Conover said, "Well, maybe I can scare you up somebody around here to do it for you. Always a few boys hangin' around, lookin' for work."

Strike considered for a moment. Then, "Never mind. Forget it. I'll swap off with my crew and we'll get by. Won't be on the trail many days. My partner square up with you for your work?"

Conover nodded. "All square. All you got to do is line out with your herd."

Strike shook Conover's hand, thanked him and rode on toward the herd. Hendrix and the others had already reached it and were awaiting his instructions. The cattle were beginning to bed down in a hollow which formed a natural corral. They should be easy to hold through the night. Hendrix had sent Longbridge and Keno Davis, with the beef they had driven from the brakes, on to the waterhole.

"Still got a hour 'til dark," Hendrix said as he rode up. "You want to move them out and get a few miles behind us before we bed them down?"

Strike said, "Might as well stay here. Couldn't make far and the boys need the rest."

He threw his glance to the slope beyond the quieting cattle. Conover and his riders were swinging back toward Galesburg, their horses moving at a canter. He spotted the wagon then and the small *remuda* the hostler had brought. He swung his attention back to Hendrix.

"Put a couple of the boys off to one side on the herd where they can watch everything. Ought to be easy with them down in a hollow, like they are. I'll go fetch the wagon and stir up a little grub for supper."

He wheeled off, hearing Hendrix give his orders: Oren Smith to a hill on the right, Thomas to a similar point of high ground on the opposite side of the bowl. He glanced to the sky. Clear overhead with a few clouds loafing around its edges. Little prospect of rain, which would be welcome, or of a thunderstorm — which certainly would not be. But if there should come a sudden storm, or something else that spooked the herd and stampeded it, the thing to do would be to head the cattle straight up and out of the hollow, northward, and let them run until they were ready to stop. It might take a bit of doing, yet six men should turn the trick. Actually, there was small chance it would come to pass but he was thinking of it nevertheless, planning emergency measures. That herd represented his dreams of the past, their fulfillment in the future. He would not risk losing it.

The chuck wagon was well provisioned and, assuming the chore for himself that first evening, he put together a good meal of fried beef, boiled potatoes, warmed-over biscuits and strong coffee. Dessert was a can of peaches for each man. They would take turns at the cooking job, he explained. All but Hendrix. It was better to keep the old rider, with his uncanny knowledge of cattle, with the herd. Oren Smith was to be the first. He would take over with breakfast the next morning.

The night passed without event and they moved out of the hollow in the cold gray before daybreak. Hendrix, riding point, with the black-and-white longhorn at the head of the column, struck a line for the north. Strike sent Longbridge and Thomas to the sides, or swing positions and Keno Davis, muttering under his breath at his ill fortune, to the drag, or follow-up. It would have been better to place two riders at the rear but this lack was partly compensated for by Strike, himself, who rode a restless patrol about the herd, keeping his watch on all points. Oren Smith, with the cavvyyard of horses haltered and on lead ropes, kept pace with the slowly moving mass in the chuck wagon, two hundred yards upwind where the dust could not touch him.

Strike had a good look at the herd that day. As Arlie had prophesied, they were not too impressive at first glance. But give them that year on Tenkiller range and they would be worth plenty at the market. The stock was all branded except for the few Hendrix and the other riders had driven out of the badlands and it looked to Jim Strike as though Arlie and Angelina had negotiated with at least a half a dozen different spreads, the marks were so varied.

He saw quite a few Slash W brand; many Lazy 7, Circle Cross, Three Bars, Walking Triangle and some he could not recognize. Riding alongside the bawling, dusty herd, he wished again Arlie had waited or, at least, had left the bills of sale for him. He had traded and driven enough cattle in his life to know the importance of having handy the proof of ownership of a herd, particularly one of mixed brands. Arlie should have realized that. But they were moving at a good pace for so large a herd. In a few more days they would be in Tenkiller country and he could forget the possibility of trouble.

Or could he?

Thinking of Arlie and the ranch brought the matter of Angelina's hostility to his mind along with certain other incidents that had occurred. He wished now he had talked more with the girl before she had departed with Arlie on the buying trip. There was a misunderstanding somewhere and he should have cleared it up before it went further. If it was a *misunderstanding!* His mind came to a full halt on that thought.

They stopped that night on a high, flat *mesa,* green with grass but with no water.

The herd was in good condition, however, and that lack did not bother them greatly. There was a large grove with good water two days further on, Strike had been told. The stock should have no trouble doing without until they reached that point.

The next day proved to be a trying one. The sun burned down from an empty, glassy sky with all the fierce intensity of mid-August and the cattle began to turn restive and belligerent. The lead bull several times attempted to turn and lead his charges back over the route they had just covered, but Aaron Hendrix succeeded in keeping him headed north, hazing him on with shouts and a doubled rope which served as a lash. The crew changed horses three times during daylight hours, and when darkness came and they bedded the stock in a long, narrow valley, they got only a small amount of rest.

The following day was no different. The herd grew harder to manage with each passing hour. It was only the thought of reaching water by sundown that cheered the crew and kept them sweating with the steers. Water would solve their problems, lighten their work.

"Never seen a bunch of cows dry out and get wall-eyed so damn fast," Longbridge remarked to Strike near the middle of the morning.

"Been plenty hot last couple of days. And they haven't had a chance to get used to the drive yet."

"Mighty glad we've got a waterhole comin' up. Don't figure we got enough crew to hold them, if ever they take it in their jug heads to turn back."

Strike nodded. "If something does get them started, we'll try to keep them pointed north. That way they'll run for the waterhole and stop when they reach it."

Longbridge spat. "That's right. Only job's goin' to be to make them run that way. That old spotted longhorn's bound to have ideas of his own."

"He makes one move to swing the herd, he gets a bullet square between the eyes."

Midday came and passed with the heat making itself felt intensely. Dust hung in a thick cloud over the herd, blinding and choking man and beast alike. Only Carl Thomas, taking his hitch with the chuck wagon and cavvyyard, rode beyond the yellowish, smothering pall.

Late in the afternoon they sighted the grove, a long, dark green band lying across the floor of a wide valley. An hour later the herd smelled the water and immediately began to quicken the pace, the old longhorn moving well out in front. Hendrix pulled off to one side, knowing the herd would not now swing from course. He galloped on ahead to look over the waterhole and soon was back.

"Good place," he told Strike, who, with the rest of the crew, had dropped back to prod any stragglers. "Smooth ground and a fair-sized pond. We won't be havin' no trouble with them now."

Strike sighed in relief. "Glad of that. Reckon we can all stand some rest and a good sleep."

"We'll get it," Hendrix said and wheeled away.

Near sundown they were there. The cattle took their fill of water and drifted on to graze and bed down on the grassy slope beyond the sink. Carl Thomas was preparing the evening meal for the weary men who were talking quietly and drinking strong coffee around the wagon.

"Don't figure we'll have any trouble tonight," Strike said to Aaron Hendrix, "but I expect we'd still better post a nighthawk. We can spell off, taking a couple hours apiece."

Hendrix nodded. "Best we take no chances. Never know what the critters will do." He lifted his gaze, a frown crossing his weathered face.

"We got company," he said in a strained voice, "and they're wearin' masks!"

CHAPTER EIGHT

There were eleven of them.

They had ridden in quietly, on the off side of the chuck wagon, unseen and unheard. They sat on their horses in a slowly forming half-circle about the camp, each man with covered face and wearing a slicker to further conceal his person. Several carried rifles, others pistols. Their leader, a man who looked vaguely familiar to Strike, moved in a step closer.

"You will keep your hands up," he stated in a matter-of-fact way. "This all the party?"

Strike immediately recognized the voice. It was the *vaquero* who had led the attempted hold-up. Only this time he was not wearing his Mexican clothing.

One of the riders behind him spoke up. "It's all of them. Six men. Counted them this mornin'."

The leader was a big man, large in his saddle. He said, "Two men stand with the herd. Don't want them to scatter."

Strike let his eyes search the group. He was looking for the blond, Calloway and his redheaded friend. He could not spot either since the light was not too good. But they could have been there, heavily masked.

"What's this all about?" he asked then, anger beginning to stir within him. "What do you want?"

"Get their guns," the *vaquero* ordered, ignoring the question. "Rifles, too."

One of the masked men dropped from his saddle. He moved in behind Strike and his crew and began to remove their weapons. Another went methodically from the gelding to each of the other horses, pulled the rifles from their saddle boots and tossed them under the wagon. This done the leader turned his attention to Strike.

"You are foreman of this herd?"

"My stock, if that's what you mean."

The big man laughed. "Hear that, *amigos?* His stock, he says. Your name is Strike?"

"Not that it's any of your business, but it is. Now, pull off that mask if you want any more answers from me. I don't talk to any man who hasn't got the guts to show his face."

The man shrugged. He said, "Do not worry about it. It will matter little, one way or another, in a few minutes."

"Meaning what?"

"Meaning we do not waste time on rustlers in this country."

"Rustlers!" Pete Longbridge, echoed, suddenly finding his voice.

Jim Strike looked closely at the *vaquero*. He had been the leader of the outlaws who had attempted the hold-up; now he was posing as the head of a posse — of vigilantes! Were the rest of the masked men outlaws, too, or were they ranchers being misled by the big man? Another question crowded into his mind: was this raid a coincidence or did it, somehow, tie in with the attempted hold-up?

Strike decided his best move was to play out the hand. He said, "If you think this is a stolen herd, you're making a mistake. This stock was bought and paid for by my partner, Arlie Silvershell. We've a spread in Tenkiller Valley. I picked up the herd at Galesburg three days ago."

In the tight, oppressive hush the *vaquero* said, "Of course. You have papers to prove it, eh?"

Strike hesitated. "Matter of fact, I haven't. Not with me. My partner went on ahead with the bills of sale. If there's doubt in your

92

mind, I'll ride with you to the ranch and get them."

The leader shrugged, laughed. He glanced over his shoulder at the others. "No papers. It would seem that we have finally found the hombres that steal our cattle. They are most sure of themselves, too. They do not even bother to rig up the papers any more."

Aaron Hendrix suddenly pushed forward, his face red and working angrily. "Now, look here, you vigilantes or whatever you are — this ain't no rustled herd! I was with Mr. Strike when he took delivery at Galesburg. You don't want to take his word, ride back there and talk to that feller, Conover. He'll tell you he turned this bunch of cows over to us."

"Conover? At Galesburg? I know no one by that name. Do any of you men?" he added, again sweeping the remainder of the posse with his glance.

There was a general denial. One rider said, "I been in this country a long time. Never heard of no man named Conover."

Pete Longbridge swore softly. "Should a knowed better than to get myself mixed up with a jinx outfit!"

Keno Davis, fear coloring his voice said, "We don't know nothin' about this. We just hired on as drovers. We ain't got nothin' to do with owin' this herd, mister!"

"Shut up, Keno," Hendrix snapped. "Reckon Mr. Strike'll straighten all this out."

"It's a fact!" Carl Thomas broke in. "I was just stallin' around a bar in Paso Largo when this man Strike come in lookin' for drovers to help him move a herd. I sure never figured to have anything to do with a rustled herd. Not me! Had I known, you wouldn't find me within ninety miles of this outfit!"

Jim Strike listened to the run of conversation with growing uneasiness. The vigilantes were paying no heed to the truth and explanations. He wished again that Arlie had left the papers covering the purchase of the stock. But even if he had, it was doubtful the masked men would have believed them genuine.

Nevertheless, it should be an easy thing to straighten out. It was ridiculous to think that it could not be! All he needed was the opportunity. Have the posse get in touch with Arlie or with Conover. Or some of the ranchers from whom the stock had been purchased. They would be the best proof. First, of course, it would be necessary to see Arlie and obtain the names of the ranchers.

He said, "This is all a waste of time. You don't want to take my word for it, send a couple of your men to my ranch and bring back my partner. He can tell you who he bought this stock from and you can verify it with them."

The masked leader shook his head. "Where did you say this ranch of yours is?"

"Tenkiller Valley."

"Tenkiller Valley? There was no ranch there the last time I rode through." He turned half about in the saddle. "*Amigos,* do you know about a ranch in Tenkiller Valley?"

There was a murmur of noes. One of the riders said, "Was there deer huntin' about three years back. Sure wasn't no ranch there then."

The calmness began to slip from Jim Strike. It was like trying to climb a sheer wall of granite; he was getting nowhere. A strange feeling came over him. The whole thing was too pat, too well worked out. The vigilantes didn't want to believe him, regardless of what he said. What was behind it all? *Who* was behind it?

Anger, and a strong sense of helplessness brought a fine sweat to his forehead. He glanced at Hendrix, Longbridge and the other men. They were silent and had been, except for the two or three who had voiced their opinions. He could sense the fear that was settling over them. But Aaron Hendrix would not remain quiet.

"You got no call to come jumpin' us like this!" he exclaimed. "We ain't rustlers and we can dang well prove it if you'll give us the chance! Now, you just send a couple of your men over to Mr. Strike's place and fetch his partner. We'll squat right here 'til they get back."

The vigilante leader chuckled. "To lessen the odds against you, old one? You mistake my intelligence. There is no ranch in Tenkiller Valley. And there is no man called Conover around Galesburg." He paused, glanced toward the sun now behind the horizon. "All right, boys, get the rope. I would have this finished by dark."

"No, by God!" Longbridge suddenly yelled and whirled for his horse. "You ain't stringin' me up!"

A rifle cracked, the sound sharp and precise in the bush. Longbridge jolted as the bullet caught him between the shoulders. He stumbled on a few staggering steps, fell headlong, his body going into a grotesque heap at the base of a tree.

There was complete silence following the shot. In those succeeding moments Jim

Strike and the men who were with him came face to face with the cold and brutal realization of what lay ahead for them. A lynching. The possibility of it had been in Strike's mind, of course, but it had been remote, lying far back and receiving little attention. Now the shock of Pete Long-bridge's death brought it into keen-edged focus. A wild sort of fury shook him. He took a long step toward the vigilante leader, ignoring the quick lifting of guns to cover him.

"That was murder! That was an innocent man you shot down! And the rest of us are just as innocent. We have a right to prove it!"

"Rustlers do not have rights," the man said coolly. "We have heard all your proof. A mixed herd, no papers. Bought from a man who is unknown and headed for a ranch that does not exist. That is very small proof, mister."

"All I ask is you hold up long enough to get in touch with my partner," Strike said, desperately. "A day at the most is all it would take. Maybe two."

"And maybe you have some friends who will arrive in that time to give you a help with the herd. That may be why you would have us wait."

Strike stared at the man's deep-set eyes. He again had that feeling that it was all some sort of fantastic, put-up job and he wondered who stood behind it. He could not believe it was Arlie.

He said, "Is there anything at all I can say or do to make you listen to me? What if we all ride to Long Pass or even Paso Largo? We can prove to you there who we are and that you're all wrong."

The big man shook his head. "These are the facts. We have caught a gang of rustlers, red-handed. We are going to string them up. That's all there is to it. We do not need to go anyplace."

"You've got your mind made up and there's nothing going to change it. That's what you really mean. Doesn't make any difference whether we're guilty or not. But there's more to this, I figure. Mind telling me who put you up to it?"

The vigilante leader, his hard eyes barely visible above his mask, only stared. Without turning his head, he said, "Where is that rope?"

One of the riders moved up beside him, a coiled lariat in his hand.

"All right, get them on their horses. The tree to the left will serve us well. Get on with it, it grows dark."

In the tense, deadly hush, Strike watched two of the men lead up his bay and the rest of the crew's mounts. He swung into the saddle, his mind struggling to come up with a solution, an answer or a plan for escape. It had to be quick. In a few more minutes they would all be dead. It was hard to comprehend, to believe that he and the men who had worked for him were actually experiencing their last few minutes of life; but they were — unless he could do something about it.

He twisted about to face the vigilante leader. "This is a mistake and you'll live to regret it. But there's no making you or any of the rest of your bunch see it. Point is, don't take it out on my men. I'm the owner of this herd and they just hired on to help. None of them ever saw me before the day I signed them on. If you've got to have blood, look to me for it. Turn them loose."

"Sure, that's right!" Carl Thomas cried out in a fearful voice. "We ain't done nothin'. We was just workin' for him!"

"Maybe that herd was rustled," Keno Davis added, "but we sure didn't know if it was. Can't blame a man for takin' a job when it's offered to him."

The *vaquero* laughed. "This will be a lesson to you, cowboy. Next time you will be more careful who you hire out to!"

"Yeh, the next time," Oren Smith murmured in bitter humor.

One of the posse members rode up behind the boy, dropped a rope loop over his head and drew it tight. Smith at once seized it with his hands and tore at it, loosening it. His eyes were spread wide in terror.

"Reckon you better figure on tying them down," one of the riders observed. "They'll be fightin' the noose all the way if we don't."

The leader said, "Get them under that tree first. We will take them one at a time."

Jim Strike watched as a rider picked up the reins of the bay gelding and started for the spreading cottonwood tree, selected for the executions. He glanced about, sweat now standing out freely on his face in bean-sized beads. There were only minutes left and they were swiftly running out.

"Wait a minute!" he suddenly yelled. "You can't do this!"

He turned about in the saddle, faced the rest of the masked riders. "This is all a framed-up job of some kind! I don't know who you men are, but if you're ranchers around here — honest ranchers — you must know my partner, Arlie Silvershell! He's been around this country for several years. And his wife — she's one of the Mondragon family from Paso Largo. You must have heard of them. You've got to look into this thing before you go any further!"

The group had come to a full halt. Strike could feel the eyes of the masked men upon him. But, hidden as their faces were, he had no way of knowing what effect, if any, his words were having upon them.

"I don't know what this man who leads you has told you, but it can't be truth. And I think you ought to know that he's an outlaw, himself. He, and four other men held me up the other day and robbed me. They didn't get much but that wasn't their fault. They just didn't know where to look. Now, does it make sense to the rest of you men that an outlaw ought to be heading up a party of law-abiding citizens?"

Strike paused again. He waited out the tense, dragging moments for comment. There was none. And again he wondered what sort of men he was speaking to — outlaws or honest ranchers.

"All I'm asking for is a chance to show you that you're all wrong. You can't hang five men on the strength of what this outlaw is passing off as evidence. You've already got one murder on your hands. Don't make it worse!"

Strike settled back, brushed at the sweat

piled thickly on his forehead. The next moment would tell the story. If there was one honest man in the masked riders, Strike was certain he would speak out. But time ran on, the silence heavy and unnerving.

Finally the *vaquero* said, "It is enough. The man has had his say. Now we go ahead."

The half-circle of masked riders moved forward. A long, gusty sigh escaped Strike's lips. He had failed to reach any of them.

CHAPTER NINE

In the closing darkness, Jim Strike and his men were led slowly toward the cotton-wood. They rode side by side, two of the masked men on foot ahead of them, guiding the horses. Behind them the remainder of the vigilantes followed silently.

Strike looked ahead. A fairly dense thicket lay a scant thirty feet beyond the broadly spreading tree. Further back of the tamarack, the grove itself offered its shadowy, deep protection. Safety and escape lay there — if they could make it. It would be a long chance but he could see no other possibilities. If they delayed much longer their hands would be bound at their backs and escape would be impossible.

He glanced to his left. Oren Smith, the rope still around his neck, his young face pale and drawn by despair in the half-light, was slumped in the saddle. To his right, Jim could see Aaron Hendrix and next to him

Keno Davis. On the outside, at the end of the line, was Carl Thomas. He carefully estimated all their chances. Slim — but possible. Darkness would be of some help and the two vigilantes ahead of them on the ground would prove helpful. Their friends would be hesitant about shooting, fearing to hit one of them.

And a few seconds was all Jim Strike asked for. Just enough to make a wild dash for the tamarack and then the grove beyond it. Perhaps they would not all make it unharmed but he knew the others would be as willing to gamble on it as he.

What worried him most was the lynch rope looped about Oren Smith's neck. Its farther end was still in the hand of a vigilante. At the first move the youngster made, the masked man only would need to haul back on the rope to drag Smith from his horse. If Oren would just have the presence of mind to quickly throw a couple of loops about his saddle horn, thus taking up the slack, he could avoid being dragged to the ground. He glanced up. The cottonwood was only steps away.

It was time to make a move — if one was to be made.

"Boys," he said then, addressing Hendrix and the rest of the crew and speaking loud so all could easily hear. "I'm sorry I got you into this. It's a raw deal we're getting, but I'm thinking one thing — I figure the same as Pete Longbridge did."

Hendrix swiveled his attention sharply to Strike. He stared briefly and then settled slowly back as understanding came to him. Oren Smith nodded, tugged at the noose about his throat, loosening it. Strike hoped that Davis and Thomas had also caught the meaning of his words.

One of the men leading the horses half-turned. "Who the hell is Pete Longbridge?"

Strike tensed in the saddle. There was no way to give a signal, no means to communicate without arousing the masked men's suspicions. He would just have to chance it, hope that the others understood and would be ready.

He said, "Man I once knew. Always said you could die just one time. But he figured it was better for a man to do his own choosing than let somebody else — now!"

He plunged spurs into the gelding's flanks. The big horse, startled, leaped forward. Beside him Strike heard a yell break from Hendrix's lips, or maybe it was Keno Davis. He was not sure. The two men ahead on the ground, dropped the reins they were holding, scrambled frantically to get from under the sudden onslaught of hoofs. A gun cracked loudly close by. A bullet sang by Strike's head, thudded into a stump a few yards away.

"Look out!" a voice shouted. "Don't hit Earl or Jamison!"

At the gelding's first leap, Strike had flung himself low over the saddle, long arms reaching down for the trailing reins. He caught them with his outstretched fingers, yelled in the bay's ear to rush on. One of the masked men was suddenly before him. The bay swerved to avoid a collision. The man was struggling to draw his pistol from beneath his slicker. Drawing his foot free of the stirrup, Strike kicked out. The heel of his boot caught the man high on the chest, bowled him over into a stand of brush.

"Get Strike!"

Jim recognized the voice of the vigilante leader. He crouched lower over the bay's neck. The thicket was only a breath away. The others of his crew were spread out alongside him. From the corner of his eye he could see Oren Smith, the rope loose and trailing behind him. He had managed to jerk it free of the hands that held it but it could easily snag in the brush and pull him from the saddle.

"Watch that rope!" he yelled at the youngster.

Keno Davis was out in front a short distance, already ducking into the tamarack. Guns were opening up behind them now. The two men on the ground were out of the line of fire. Strike kept low, constantly urging the bay to run, prodding the horse with his spurs. He could hear the vicious sounds of bullets clipping through the brush, thudding into tree trunks or striking branches and whining off shrilly into the night.

"Forget the rest of them — get Strike!"

Again it was the voice of the vigilante leader. Strike grinned into the darkness. He was the prime target — just why, he would be greatly interested in knowing.

He felt a sudden wrench at his left shoulder. There was a white-hot, burning sensation. He had been hit. They reached the tamarack and plunged into its depths. To his right Aaron Hendrix was curving in toward him, his face set and drawn.

"You hit?" the old rider yelled.

"Not bad!" Strike shouted back. "Keep on going. Scatter out!"

Hendrix swung away, his black horse laboring hard. Beyond him the vague, indefinite shapes of two other riders were fading into the thick shadows. That would be Davis and Carl Thomas. They would likely make it if their madly running horses did not stumble in their wild flight.

His shoulder felt numb and wet. It was not a serious wound, he knew. One that would probably bleed considerably, but it would not prove dangerous. He was no stranger to bullet wounds. There had been two occasions before when he had known the shocking impact of lead, both times in far more serious locations than this. As soon as he got a chance he would pad the wound and stop the flow of blood. The bullet had gone on through. It did not have that tight, swelled feeling that a piece of lead, imbedded in flesh, always gave.

The shooting had ceased. Behind him the vigilantes were spreading out, beginning a serious, methodic pursuit. Strike swung the bay, now blowing somewhat, to his left, going deeper into the shadowy depths of the grove. He caught a glimpse of a rider directly across from him. It was the boy, Oren Smith. The rope no longer trailed out behind him. Strike grinned his relief. Oren had made it. Now, if he and all the others could keep out of sight for another few minutes, complete darkness would enable them to escape entirely. Too bad Pete Longbridge had not waited. He had made his belief in a jinx come true.

His shoulder began to throb dully as the anesthetic of shock gradually wore off. The bay's steady running, broken now and then with a jolt as he momentarily halted or veered to miss some object that loomed unexpectedly in his path, kept the wound bleeding freely.

A sudden burst of gunshots back and to the right brought a frown to Strike's strained features. The vigilantes apparently had caught sight of one of the crew, just which one he could only guess. Hendrix, Davis and Thomas were all over in that direction, somewhere.

He pulled the bay down to a fast walk, listening intently for sounds directly to his rear. He could hear nothing. The posse seemed to be farther off to the right. His gradual swinging away had carried him out of their path. A thick stand of some sort of brush rose up dead ahead. He guided the bay in behind it and halted, listening again. The only sounds to be heard above the harsh sucking of the gelding, were those far off to the north; men shouting, faint and indistinguishable.

He pulled the bandana from around his neck, snapped it sharply to dislodge the accumulated dust. He ran his right hand under his shirt, feeling for the wound. It was somewhere below his shoulder bone. The area was numb and stiff. He could not determine exactly where the bullet had entered, at first, but finally he located the place. The lead had caught only the flesh. He worked the makeshift bandage under his shirt, wrapped it around his upper arm loosely and then forced it back until it covered the wound. It was a difficult place to bandage but when he was done, after several minutes of hard, sweating work that left him gasping for breath, the cloth was over the hole and the bleeding was stanched to some degree.

He sat on the gelding, listening again for the posse. He could no longer hear them and this set up a small worry within him. They could either be going away, striking for a different, opposing direction — or they could be filtering silently in toward him. At least when he could hear them he had some idea as to where they were. Now there was no way of telling. He considered his next move.

He was fairly certain Hendrix and the other members of his crew had gotten away, unless that last spatter of gunshots had meant something. The vigilantes concentrating upon him had enabled Hendrix and the others to split up and quickly lose themselves in the grove's darkness. He figured he need worry no more about any of them, only about himself now.

He concluded his next, most logical move would be to head for the ranch. There he could talk things over with Arlie, see if there was more to this raid by so-called vigilantes than appeared on the surface. And he could get medical attention for his shoulder there, also. Then, with Arlie and the men who were working at the ranch, he could muster a small posse of his own and swing back. They could overtake the herd before it could be moved very far.

He waited out another five minutes, carefully checking his position and getting his bearings while he did so. The ranch would be to the north. That was not so good. That was where he had last heard sounds of the masked men. He would have to proceed carefully since they likely were working their way through the grove, hoping to find one or more of their intended victims hiding in the brush.

He put the gelding into motion, keeping to the well-shadowed pools and darkened lanes between trees. It would be a long ride to the ranch and an uncomfortable one, as his shoulder had settled down to a steady, thudding pain. But he was not complaining. He felt fortunate to be alive at all.

He rode slowly for the better part of a half-hour, taking care to keep the gelding from making any more noise than was absolutely necessary. Full night had closed in and it was difficult to see clearly all that lay in their path; low bushes, wind-banked piles of dead leaves that rattled dryly when the bay's feet came up against them, fallen limbs that popped loudly when the horse came down upon them with his weight.

Even so, it was the bay that first caught the sound. Or perhaps it was the smell of another horse that brought him to a pricked-ear attention. His head snapped up. He halted in strike. Jim Strike was instantly alert. He had no weapon of any sort with which to fight. He had no choice but to nudge the gelding gently into a deeper shadow and wait, hoping the animal would not give them away with a burst of nickering.

Faint starlight had begun to filter down through the leaves, dappling the shrubbery and forest floor. Somewhere back to the south a night bird began to call, a forlorn, empty sound that heightened the loneliness of the silent grove. Then Strike heard the slow approach of a horse. It was coming directly toward them. He glanced desperately about, seeking some kind of weapon. There was nothing. Not even a limb stout enough to serve as a club. He waited out the moments, and watched.

The horse came into a patch of light. The rider was doubled forward in the saddle, his hat gone, arms dangling loosely at either side of his mount's neck. Only the rigidity of the man's legs was keeping him in the saddle. In the next instant Jim Strike recognized the injured rider.

Aaron Hendrix.

CHAPTER TEN

Strike waited until Hendrix's horse was directly opposite. He had to take care and not frighten the animal and send him plunging erratically off into the night.

"Whoa, boy," he called out softly.

The black's head came up with a jerk. He stopped abruptly. Hendrix's body shifted dangerously at the move. Strike spoke again to the horse, keeping his voice low and soothing. He slid from the saddle and, looping the reins over a bush, he moved by the bay, toward the nervous black. When he was close enough he reached out and swiftly seized the leathers which Hendrix had hung about the horn before he lost consciousness. Strike immediately drew the black alongside the gelding.

He tarried a few moments, listening for indications of pursuit. Apparently no one had been following Hendrix for he heard nothing. He pulled the old rider's feet from the stirrups and lifted him down, laid him flat on the humus-covered earth. His shoulder leaped and throbbed from the effort but he paid little attention to it.

Hendrix struggled to open his eyes, bright with pain and fever already setting in. He stared at Strike, scarcely recognizing him in the murky light.

"That you, Mr. Strike?" he asked with a weak grin. "Guess we made it. You know about the others?"

"They made it, far as I know," Jim replied. "Now you button up while I take a look at that hole in your back."

He carefully turned Hendrix over onto his stomach, impatient with the pain in his own body. The back of the man's shirt was sodden with blood, now soaking through his vest. The bullet had torn a large, ragged hole just below the shoulder blade and the lead was still somewhere inside Hendrix, since there was no wound in the breast. Aaron needed a doctor and needed one very soon. The nearest would be in Long Pass, a full day or more away. Strike, a stranger to the country, could not be sure just how far.

He would have to get the old rider there. It did not occur to him that it was a near impossible task which could cost him his own life, or that Hendrix would probably not survive such a grueling ride. Nor did he consider that by taking the man to Long Pass instead of going on to the ranch in Tenkiller Valley, as he had planned, he would be jeopardizing his chances for recovering the lost herd. He was thinking of one thing only — Aaron Hendrix and his need for medical attention.

But before they could go anywhere, Hendrix must be attended to. Strike got to his feet. He needed something for bandage. He glanced at his own shirt. It was heavy, coarse material and would be of little value for such purpose. He moved to the black Hendrix had been riding and dug into the saddlebags. After a moment, he came up with a clean pair of white drawers. They were of a knit cotton and did not tear easily, but with the aid of a sharp knife he eventually had several strips of cloth that would serve the need.

He worked in feverish haste, fully aware of the passing time, placing pads at the wound opening, binding them into place with his improvised bandages. He found an old, well-worn brush jacket rolled up in Hendrix's blanket and this he put on the faintly groaning man. The night would grow cold before daylight came again and Hendrix was certain to chill from the wound's reaction.

His own nagging injury was bothering him little. No more than a persistent drawing and plucking and he refused to heed it. Only when he lifted Hendrix to the saddle did he become aware that it still bled steadily, that he was losing more blood than was good for him. He readjusted the bandage and then secured Hendrix to the black by tying his feet into the stirrups and anchoring them with a stout rope running under the black's belly.

Hendrix was vaguely conscious, mumbling and protesting incoherently most of the time, but when Strike thrust the black's reins into his hands, his gnarled fingers tightened about the leather strips and he endeavored to sit straighter in the saddle. Strike grinned at the old rider's nerve and swung onto his own horse. It would have been better to allow Hendrix some rest before starting on the ride to Long Pass but it would also have been dangerous. The vigilantes might turn up at any moment and Aaron had to have a doctor as quickly as possible.

He wheeled about and headed due east, knowing the town would lay somewhere in that direction. A bit more to the south, he reckoned, but he could correct that later.

For the present, it would be wise to keep well within the protective cover of the trees and shrubbery of the grove. Hendrix's black did not lead well at first. He held back, his long head flattened out at the drag of the short rope Strike had attached to the bit ring. But before the first mile had been covered, he got the idea, moved up a step or two closer to the bay and trailed docilely along, giving Strike no more trouble.

At the end of an hour Strike halted. He dismounted and walked back to have a look at Hendrix. The old rider was still grimly erect in the saddle, head sunk forward on his chest. The bandage, purposely drawn tight, was keeping the flow of blood checked and lending some support to his weakening body. Strike loosened the cloth strips for a brief time and then, after checking the ropes around Hendrix's ankles to assure himself they had not worked loose, he reset the bandages and returned to the bay.

They were drawing near the edge of the grove. He had begun to notice a gradual thinning of the brush, fewer trees. He glanced to the sky. It was clear and a strong moon and bright stars were flooding the land with a silvery, foglike radiance. Two men on horseback would easily be seen by anyone watching the flat plains country.

They would have to chance that. They must get away from the grove while it was still night and be as far from it as possible before daylight came. Strike reached back over his left shoulder, felt the pad he had placed over his wound. It was in place but thick with warm, sticky blood. That disturbed him. It seemed to him the wound should have stopped bleeding by now.

He resumed the flight, Hendrix's black now willing and co-operative. He wished he was better acquainted with the country. If only he knew of a long valley or even a fairly deep swale into which they could ride after they broke out of the grove, they could keep below the flat, long running skyline and not become silhouetted so distinctly for all to see. He racked his memory, trying to recall the land he had crossed traveling from Long Pass to the ranch. It had all been level most of the way, with only a few ravines and hollows of any consequence. Anyway, they were many miles west of that route.

Quite suddenly his flagging senses leaped to a keen alertness. Somewhere off to the left a sound had broken through the night's natural noises. He halted the bay with a light pressure of his knees. Behind him Hendrix's black came to a stop. A groan escaped the old rider's thin lips at the sudden cessation of motion. Silently, Jim Strike slipped from his saddle and stepped back to the injured man's side. The horses likely would make no sound. They were too tired to move about needlessly and having each other for company, they would not nicker. It was Aaron Hendrix who could unwittingly give them away, should it be one of the vigilantes approaching.

They were almost out in the open, in the half-light of the moon and stars. It could not be helped now. It was too late to move. Cursing his luck for having no weapon of any sort, Strike stood at the side of the suffering Hendrix and waited out the tense, dragging moments. The sounds were growing louder, drawing nearer. He could distinguish them now; the slow, methodic hoofbeats of a tired horse, possibly two of them, the faint creak of leather and light, musical jingle of bridle metal. It was off to the left, not far. Frozen, Jim Strike waited. He had no weapon, to be sure, but he still had his two hands — and the desperate desire to stay alive.

The sounds ceased. Strike held his position. Whatever, or whoever, he had heard, was only a few feet away. A sudden orange flare of light broke a pool of blackness in the night. Turning his head gently, he located the source. A rider, one of the vigilantes, astride his horse, twenty, perhaps thirty feet distant. He had paused to light a cigarette. The fragrant, tantalizing odor of the burning tobacco drifted to Strike.

Strike watched the small, red glow brighten and diminish alternately as the man puffed at his cigarette. He was growing tired, cramped from standing rigidly, half-turned, for so long. Hendrix stirred restlessly. Strike prayed for the rider to move on. Their luck could not hold for much longer.

As if in answer, the coal of the cigarette was suddenly gone. The shape of the man on the weary horse began to materialize as he started forward. He drew nearer. Strike tensed himself for a sudden move, a wild lunge at the man designed to knock him from his saddle, tumble him to earth. He must get his hands on the man's throat at the onset to prevent his crying out. The rest of the posse might not be far away. Not daring to move, Strike hung on. Unless the man changed his direction, he would ride straight into the clearing where they stood.

And then the vigilante was broadside, going away. A silent sigh of relief flooded through Strike. In the next instant the rider was gone from view. He had swung off into the deep brush, apparently following out some precut trail that wound off to the south. Strike's bunched muscles relaxed, smoothed out. He waited out another two minutes, giving the man ample time to get well beyond earshot. Then he walked back to the bay. That had been close.

He stepped into the saddle and started forward. He covered no more than a dozen steps when a voice challenged him from the shadows.

"Domino? That you?"

Aaron Hendrix groaned in feverish pain at the halt. The bay shook his head at the tight rein, creating sound. Strike sat completely still.

"Hey, Domino!"

From off behind Strike, along the trail the first rider had followed, came the answer.

"Yeh? What you want?"

There was a long silence. Then, "Nothin'. I heard somethin' over that way. Reckon it must have been you."

"Well, I'm sure over here," Domino replied, "so don't you go takin' no pot shots in this direction."

Jim Strike's heavy shoulders went down in an exhausted expression of mitigation. Suddenly and unaccountably he felt the solid drag of weariness. He listened dully to the scrape and thud as the second vigilante passed in front of him somewhere, hidden from view by the brush. He did not immediately move even after all was still. It was good just to sit, to rest. His eyes were heavy and it was a great effort to do more than stay upright in the saddle.

He came to with a start. He had been dozing and that alarmed him. He shouldn't have been sleepy. It must be the wound, he decided, sapping his strength and fogging his mind. He glanced at Hendrix. The old rider was slumped in the saddle, hands folded over the horn, locked tight together. His face was abnormally pale and transparent in the ghostly light.

Strike touched the bay with spurs, starting him forward. The gelding was not so anxious to move now, fatigue dragging at him, also. They traveled forward a hundred yards or so and were at once at the edge of the grove. Strike halted again and looked out upon the wide, running flats and swells of the plains. It was beautiful under the clear glow of the moon and starlight, but it offered little protection.

It occurred to him then that they could, conceivably, have gotten beyond the vigilantes. It was entirely possible the posse had been riding in a circle through the grove, searching in a wide, forage-line fashion; that he and Hendrix had, by mere chance, blundered through an opening in that line. The last man they had encountered, and almost ridden into, could have been the outmost member of the searching party. If such were true, there should be no one else around. It was logical but he would not accept it without some manner of proof.

He slid from the bay, anchored him to a small cedar tree and moved off through the brush. He covered a hundred yards up the edge of the grove, listening and probing the shadows carefully. He found no one — nothing. He retraced his steps, followed a like procedure in the opposite direction. Again he saw no signs of the posse.

Confident now that he was right, he returned to the gelding, mounted up, and with Hendrix folded forward over the saddle of his black, he rode boldly out of the concealing shadows onto the *mesa*. They could make for better speed outside the hindering trees and brush and this they badly needed. Time, for Aaron Hendrix, was steadily running out.

Daylight found them far to the east, traveling the soft floor of a sandy wash. The horses were dead tired and moving slowly. Hendrix was a senseless shape on the black, swaying and weaving with the motion of his mount, remaining in the saddle only because of the ropes that bound him to it.

Near mid-morning they reached a small scatter of wild olive trees, offering some degree of shade and coolness. There was no spring, but Strike knew his canteen was almost full. He pulled to a stop. The horses must have some rest, as well as Hendrix and himself. He untied the ropes that fixed the old rider to his saddle and laid him out on the ground in the deepest of the filigree shade.

Taking the canteen, he forced a swallow between the man's pinched lips and then had a drink himself. He turned to the horses and loosened the cinches, but did not remove their gear. Hendrix's canteen also was near full and he watered the two animals, using his hat as a pail. There wasn't enough water to satisfy either the bay or the black but it helped and quieted them considerably. He tied them securely so they would not wander off and when he started back to Hendrix, they both had already begun to graze about and nibble contentedly at the thin grass growing along the edge of the wash.

Bone weary from the long hours of tension and slow riding, weakened by the loss of blood from his wound, he staggered slightly as he walked. He reached Hendrix, sleeping a deathlike slumber, and dropped beside him. After a moment, he stretched out on the sand and closed his eyes.

He awakened to the sound of gravel crunching. He lay still, endeavouring to pinpoint the noise. It came again. Then he saw it was the gelding, moving in nearer, his black quivering lips searching over the ground for more grass. Strike sat up quickly and turned his attention to Hendrix. The man was still unconscious or sleeping, he could not tell which; his face was flushed and he stirred fitfully, faint gurglings in his throat. Strike looked toward the west. About an hour until sundown. They should be on their way again.

He got up, swaying a bit as a nauseating dizziness swept through him like a wall of water. He shook his head savagely, seeking to clear it and throw off the thin fog that veiled his eyes. The canteen lay nearby and he flung it to his dry lips, took a drink of its tepid contents. This helped some. Then he caught up the bay's picket rope and drew him in.

He tightened the cinches and prepared him for traveling. The black, contrary as ever, was harder to get ready, but he managed it. The next task was to get Hendrix aboard. Ordinarily it would have been a simple, easy chore, but now Jim Strike discovered it took every ounce of his strength to boost the frail body into the saddle. And when it was finally done, he sagged weakly against the black, clinging to the horn while he sucked deep for breath.

It was infuriating to find himself in such straits. He clung to the black, cursing himself unreasonably, refusing to accept the fact that his own wound and resultant loss of blood had cost him dearly; that a lack of food and rest were aggravating and speeding his own physical decline. He would not believe he was scarcely able to take care of himself much less the near lifeless figure of Aaron Hendrix and he went doggedly about preparing for the remainder of the journey to Long Pass with a grim, set jaw.

Eventually, he had things ready and they once more were underway. They had reached country familiar to him now, that part of the land he crossed going to and from the town and ranch. He headed the gelding for the town and settled himself deep in the saddle, content to doze and let the horse have his head.

Sometime later he remembered Hendrix and twisted painfully around to look at the man. Through a gray haze that had settled over the country, he noted that Hendrix had bowed forward in the saddle again. Strike muttered a few incoherent words of encouragement to him and came back about.

He lost all conception of time, of distance, and somewhere during the passage of hours he became aware that the bay no longer moved; that he had stopped. He struggled to get his eyes open, hoping to determine their whereabouts. A vaguely familiar building was before him but there was no daylight left and it was very dark.

He wrapped his hands around the saddle horn to steady himself and started to dismount. Suddenly he felt himself falling, saved himself by clinging to the steel post. He shook his head, trying to focus his eyes on the building, on the door before him. He gathered his strength, walked toward it, almost steady. It seemed a long way but he reached it. Knotting his hand into a fist, he pounded at the wooden panel. There was no response and he repeated the hammering which sent sharp slivers of pain racing through his body.

The door opened. He said, "Sorry. But I'm needing a little help. My friend, there —"

As if from a great distance he heard Hannah's voice cry, "Jim — you've been hurt!"

CHAPTER ELEVEN

The first thing Jim Strike saw when he opened his eyes was the calm, serene face of Hannah Moore. He had the distinct impression of having felt the brush of her lips against him, and he could still smell the sweet, womanly fragrance of her nearness. She saw his lids open and smiled down at him.

"Welcome back." She turned away from him, disappeared into an adjoining room. She was back in a few seconds with a bowl of steaming liquid and a spoon. She sat down on the edge of the bed and began to feed him.

"It's a relief to see you swallow my broth consciously," she said. "For two days and nights I've been forcing it down you." He stared at her in astonishment. "Two days and nights!" he echoed. He glanced about the room, a frown corrugating his brow. They were in the rear of her shop. "I've been here that long?"

She pressed another spoonful of the rich, creamy soup between his lips and remembrance flooded back. He pulled himself half up in the bed.

"Hendrix? The man who was with me?" Hannah said, "I'm sorry, Jim. He is dead. It happened around noon yesterday. They had to bury him this evening."

Strike sank back onto his pillow. "Dead," he muttered bitterly. "If I could have just got him to a doctor sooner."

Hannah shook her head. "Wouldn't have mattered. He was badly hit. The bullet had lodged in his lung and there was nothing we could do for him. How do you feel?"

"Good," he said automatically, without thinking. He recalled then his own wound and gingerly moved his left shoulder and arm. There was a slight stiffness but no sharp pain. "Good," he said again. "You and the doctor did a fine job on me."

"There's no doctor around," she replied. "Only Hester. She helps when the babies are born and takes care of the men's injuries if they're too bad for home treatment." Hannah paused, smiled at him. "I think it was the first time she's ever been called on to treat a bullet wound. What happened, Jim?"

He told her, giving her the details from

the moment he and his crew had left her place after breakfast that morning to his last, flagging seconds of consciousness at her door. Anger built steadily within him while he talked. When he had finished, he was sitting upright in the bed.

"Two men dead that I know of," he said, his jaw set and showing whitely at the corners. "Maybe more. All because I couldn't make those masked fools believe me!"

"Maybe they were rustlers, themselves," Hannah offered in her quiet way. "It appears to me they didn't want to believe anything you told them."

"It's possible. And there's something else," he added, thoughtfully, his mind turning to Angelina. He did not go further into that but said, "Main thing, I've got to get on my feet and start looking for them. They'll pay for Hendrix and Longbridge and any of the others they've murdered. I'll see them all hang before I'm done with it!" She placed her hands against his breast and firmly pushed him back onto the bed. "Of course. But not until you've had more rest. You aren't able to ride yet."

"I'm all right," he insisted. "Just get me some black coffee. That's all I need."

She did not move from her place on the

bed. "What will you do?"

"Have a talk with your town marshal. See if I can get him to make up a posse and ride out with me."

"There's no marshal here," she answered. "The elders look after such things if they pertain to the settlement. If not, they believe in minding their own business. They won't help you. And the closest lawman is in Mesilla or El Paso."

"Too far," he murmured. "Time I rode there and back, that bunch could have the herd moved clear out of the country and be gone, themselves."

He remembered the deputy U.S. Marshal in Paso Largo, that day he had caught up with Chris Calloway, but he dismissed any hopes from that source. He would have a difficult time convincing the lawman of his need. Most likely he had departed anyway; Paso Largo, probably, was just a pause en-route to some other point.

"Best thing will be to go on to the ranch, like I planned at the start," he said, thinking aloud. "Let Arlie know all that's happened. Then we can scratch up a posse of our own men and start looking."

He glanced to the window, covered now by a thick, oilcloth blind. "What time of day is it?"

"After dark," she replied. "Do you still want that coffee?"

He nodded. "The stronger the better," he said.

She left the room and he immediately sat up. His clothing lay draped across a straight-backed chair and he swung about, placed his feet on the floor and reached for it. The sudden movement set his head to spinning briefly but he brushed the giddiness aside. He drew on his pants, his socks and boots. He was looking for his shirt when Hannah returned with the steaming brew.

She halted in the doorway. Her smile faded from her lips when she saw him. "Jim — you're in no condition to ride. It will be dangerous for you to try. Please — won't you wait, at least until morning? If you should run into some of those masked men —"

He shook his head, grinned. "Don't worry. There are certain things that must be done, Hannah. You must understand that."

He stood quietly in the center of the room. He was a powerful man with an immense animal vitality, and strength was returning to his whip-lean body with each passing minute. He moved his arms about, experimentally, the corded muscles rippling across his bare, browned torso.

"I'll be fine. Been through worse than this before."

He gave her a reassuring smile and took the coffee from her hands. He tipped it to his mouth, took a deep swallow and sighed gustily. "Best medicine a man can take! You any idea what happened to my shirt?"

She turned away silently and went into the next room. She came back holding the garment, washed, mended and ironed. He took it from her and pulled it on, favoring the injured shoulder slightly.

She noted this, moved her head slowly. "You should not try to ride," she said, not at all convinced.

"Be all right. Just a little touchy. Your Hester is a better doctor than I've ever come up against before. Besides, I've placed you in a bad position, staying here. Your people will not think much of it."

She shrugged, placed the empty coffee cup on a nearby washstand. "I've done nothing wrong or that I should be ashamed of. You came to me for help and I gave it. If that is wrong, then our beliefs are wrong."

"It's what people read into such as this that causes the trouble," he said, soberly. "I won't allow myself to bring it upon you."

She looked up at him, her face calm, her eyes the deep blue of a midnight sky. "It doesn't matter, Jim, what anyone thinks of me — us. All that counts is that you are all right, if you are."

"I am," he stated flatly.

"For a time yesterday and last night, I had my worries. You were so feverish and so restless and out of your head." She stopped, her face expressionless. "Jim, who is Angelina?"

He glanced at her, startled. "Angelina? Did I say something about her?"

"You did a great deal of muttering. She must have been on your mind."

He nodded. "I guess that's true."

Hannah waited a time. Then, "Have you known her very long?"

He realized immediately he had spoken little of Arlie and Angelina to her. He said, "Never got around to telling you much about things. She's my partner's wife. Spanish and very beautiful. I met her only a few days ago."

"Is — is there anything between you?"

He looked at her sharply, finding something in her words that disturbed him. "If you mean personal, there's nothing. She's Arlie's wife and that ends it. But if you are thinking of trouble, I'm not right sure. I seem to sense a feeling of some sort. Like I was not welcome, not wanted."

"Has she said anything?"

He shook his head. "Nothing. And I tried to talk to her, before they left on that buying trip, but didn't get very far. She just sort of passes it off. I'd like to know what it's all about."

"How does your partner — Arlie — act? Do you think he feels the same way?"

"Arlie's just like he always was. And he seems all fired up about the partnership." Strike paused, considered for a long minute. "No, whatever it is, he doesn't know about it. It's something she has sticking in her craw. Soon as I get a chance I'm going to get it out of her."

Hannah moved slowly to the dresser. "Is she so beautiful?"

Strike shrugged, wondering what he had said while he was feverish. There was something between them, a difference, a slow contention, and he did not like it. A bit stiffly, he said, "A beautiful woman, yes. But it means nothing. Not to me, anyway. Believe that."

He saw relief spread through her, slacken the tautness of her shoulders. He moved to her side, placed his arm about her.

"I don't know what you've been thinking but if it has anything to do with her, forget it. I've found the woman for me — you."

She came around swiftly. He closed his arms around her, drew her close. She went to the tips of her toes and pressed a kiss against his lips.

"Oh, Jim, you don't know what it means to me to hear you say that! I was afraid, so afraid —"

"Don't ever be afraid of something like that!" he said, his voice low and stern. "You'll never have cause."

She clung tightly to him for a long time and then, smiling, turned away. "If you will leave, I'd better fix you some supper. I'll get it ready while you go for your horse. He's in the stable behind the hotel."

"Good," he said. "And I'll need a gun. Any place around here where I can buy one?"

She thought for a moment. "The store is closed now. I doubt if they would have one anyway. Wait — I have an old shotgun. It belonged to my husband. You are welcome to it." She stepped into a closet, produced the double-barreled weapon. There were only three shells.

He took the gun from her, checked its mechanism. It was in working order. "This will do fine, until I can get to the ranch. Got an extra pistol in my bedroll there." He picked up his hat, stared out the window.

"Had I better use the back way, just in case there's some of your people watching?"

"The front," she said without hesitation. "It doesn't matter to me what others think."

He grinned, kissed her lightly on the cheek and went out into the dark street.

CHAPTER TWELVE

Jim Strike rode slowly across the broad plains, flooded now with a warm, silver brilliance. It would be hard to tell Arlie that he had lost their herd; it would be a terrible blow to both their hopes and unless they were fortunate enough to recover some of the stock, they could forget their plans for building their ranch into a fine spread.

Finding the cattle would not be easy after the elapse of several days and nights. Likely the raiders broke the herd up into several small jags, thereby making it easier for them to travel faster and disappear more quickly in the vast country. He had been careful not to reveal his inner feelings to Hannah, not wishing to worry her. Of course, he had been unable to pass over the encounter with the vigilantes or rustlers, whichever they were, but he had let it drop there. He had not mentioned the attempted hold-up and the fact that the *vaquero* had been the leader of both incidents. Nor that there were several other puzzling matters that needed explanation.

He wondered what he had said about Angelina while he lay on Hannah's bed and tossed restlessly in the clutches of fever. She had been cautious in telling him, saying only that he had raved on at some length. Someday he would find out — after he had squared matters for Hendrix and Longbridge and knew where he stood with Arlie on the ranch. He wanted himself free of all outside pressures and obligations before he married Hannah.

He would persuade her to tell him all and then explain the things he might have said that disturbed her and left doubts within her. It was never good for something to stand between a man and his wife; no old memories, no suspicions however groundless, no unanswered questions. The past must be the past but with no hidden shadows.

He had not asked Hannah to marry him that evening although the desire had been close to expression several times. But there was no future for him at the moment. There were too many matters that first must be resolved, too many chores that had to be attended. And Jim Strike was no fool, unaware of danger. A widow's grief had been Hannah's lot once in her young life. He would not have it so again.

It had been almost midnight when he took his leave and rode out of Long Pass on the gelding, now lively and anxious to run after his rest in the hotel's stable. There had been no point in starting the journey earlier or in now hurrying. At his present rate, he should arrive at the ranch around daybreak, which would be about right.

Far off to the east a coyote choir was practicing its discordant hymnals, the high, erratic stutter of barks on one hill taken up and echoed in slow succession by other members along the far-flung chain. Night lay across the hills and plains in a velvet-soft sheen and there was only the faintest breath of summer wind moving gently through the grass, nodding the desert flower and spreading their odd, musky fragrance. One day, perhaps, a man could enjoy and appreciate it all without the problems of bitter accounting laying upon his mind. But it could be a day far distant.

In those waning minutes before sunrise, when the night, seemingly reluctant to surrender to the bright hours, throws its finest and sharpest light into the eastern sky, Jim Strike reached the butte-guarded entrance to Tenkiller Valley country. There he came to an abrupt halt, his eyes on the ground, his heavy brows puckered into a deep and wondering frown.

A wide cattle trail, plainly marked by thousands of hoofprints, crossed the opening to the valley and wound toward the flats to the west. A large herd had passed that way not more than a day ago. A herd that numbered hundreds.

A mixture of perplexity and anger moved through him; anger at the realization that the men who were responsible for the deaths of Hendrix and Pete Longbridge and the theft of the herd could be nearby — wonder at their audacity in driving the purloined stock straight up and onto the flats where the few steers owned by Arlie and himself were grazing. It could prove the point, he admitted, that the rustlers or vigilantes actually were unaware of the ranch in Tenkiller and did not know of the small jag of steers on the flats.

Somehow it did not satisfy him. He reached down and drew the shotgun he had borrowed from Hannah out of the saddle boot. He broke it, checked its twin chambers to assure himself it was loaded and ready. Then, resting it across the horn, he started up the long, gradual slope for the flats, following the cattle trail. It was as wide and definite as the main street in Paso Largo.

An hour later he gained the crest and there swung northward, keeping to a course that paralleled the valley, now far below and to his right. Another half-hour and he caught his first sight of the herd just stirring in the deep hollow where they had bedded for the night. A column of blue smoke snaked skyward from the position some yards west of the cattle, marking the location of the cowboys' camp.

Strike, cautious, drifted in toward the herd from its eastern flank. It was large and he scanned it closely, seeking to assure himself that it was the same he had left Galesburg with. The steers were up, moving about, beginning to graze. There were no riders placed at strategic corners around the stock for there was small need of any. Cattle, on such excellent grazing land, would not move far.

He rode the full length of the hollow unnoticed and there at the end, halted. He saw the answer to the question standing not a hundred feet away; the spotted longhorn bull Hendrix and the others had hazed from the brakes. He was still at the head of the herd, still the unchallenged leader. And there were others Strike recognized; the blue with one broken-off horn, the all-white with a jet-black head. It was his herd. There was no doubt of it.

Strike's hand tightened about the stock of the shotgun. A prudent man, taking all things into consideration, would turn and make for the ranch where sufficient aid could be mustered to capture the cowboys, now squatted about their fire, drinking coffee. But Strike, a loner from the beginning, had never learned to depend upon others. The time for action, to his way of thinking, was at the moment a problem presented itself, not later.

He took a long and careful survey of the terrain, brightening now with the rising sun. By swinging wide, he saw he could circle the herd and come in on the cowboys unseen. He had been unable to determine how many men were present. But it didn't matter greatly to him in those passing seconds. If they were the same masked men who had taken the herd from him before, he could count on there being upwards of a dozen.

That did not worry him. He knew men well — and the effect a double-barreled shotgun, leveled at them, had upon their minds and courage. A crowd-killer quickly evened the odds and the influence of one man, so fortified, had the governing possibilities of a cavalry detachment.

He made the wide circuit and when he was opposite the plume of smoke, he dismounted. He tied the bay to a clump of brush and, bending low, made his way to the lip of the basin. When he reached its edge, he removed his hat, dropped flat on his belly and wormed his way to where he could peer over the rim.

Five men were hunched about the fire. Three of them Strike had never seen before but the remaining two certainly were most familiar; Francisco Vaca and another ranch hand named Tom Antrim, whom he had met the morning before leaving for Long Pass to hire a trail crew. Astonished by what he saw, Strike watched and then pulled back below the summit to consider. Their own crew must be tending the herd and that could mean only one thing — Arlie, somehow, had recovered the stolen herd.

And to prove the point the laconic voice of Tom Antrim carried to him. "We'll move the critters up about five miles. Mr. Silvershell said we was to hold them there until he gives us the word to move them again."

Strike, relief soothing through him like a cool stream, moved back to the ridge and once again looked down upon the patch-work quilt of color that was their herd. Antrim and the other men had mounted up and were swinging away toward the cattle, splitting apart to take up positions for starting the drift. They were going away from him and did not see him standing there. After a short time, he turned and walked slowly back to the bay. The deep worry and disappointment over his loss of the herd was now gone, wiped away. All that remained now was to settle things with Angelina.

He stepped to the saddle and headed the gelding once again toward the valley. He did not curve back to the buttes but stuck diagonally across the *mesa,* intending to follow the trail he had previously used in the wall of the valley. It had been steep, cutting through a ravine that gashed the west slope, but it could be traveled if done with care. He could see little sense in swinging all the distance to the valley's natural opening lying miles to the south.

He negotiated the trail without difficulty, letting the bay take his time and pick his own footing. He reached the floor of the valley at a point west of, and somewhat behind, the ranch houses and there turned northward. Minutes later he rode into the yard from the rear of the barn and halted at the corral. He was looping the reins about the log bar when the hostler emerged from the stable.

The man pulled up short, startled, and stared at Strike. Surprise blanked his swarthy face. Strike grinned at him.

"Arlie — Mr. Silvershell in the house?" he asked, pulling the shotgun from the scabbard.

The hostler brushed at his eyes, stammered. "No, *señor.* He is gone." He looked more closely at Strike. "He think you dead, *señor.* He go to see."

"How long ago?"

The hostler frowned, not understanding.

"When? When did he go away?"

The Mexican nodded. "Only five minutes."

Strike said, "Good," and started for the main house. He would exchange the shotgun for a pistol, grab a bite to eat and go after Arlie. It would not be hard to overtake him.

He reached the corner of the long, rambling structure. At that moment he heard the distinct jingle of spurs as a man came across the hard pack of the yard. He halted, wondering if it could be Arlie, returning for some reason. He moved back a step, threw his glance along the rear of the building. A saddled horse stood behind a tool shed some yards off to one side. It was not the sorrel Arlie usually rode. At that moment the rider came into the open, walking swiftly toward the side door which opened into the house. He was a big man. He looked familiar.

In that next moment Jim Strike recognized him. He saw the bullet-torn hat, the dark, hard-surfaced eyes. He had a quick vision of the man in a *vaquero* outfit, astride a horse, his face masked, a yellow slicker covering his body. There was no mistake. He was the same man.

CHAPTER THIRTEEN

A surge of hatred swept through Jim Strike. He brought the shotgun up swiftly, prepared to step out into the yard and challenge the *vaquero*. And then some inner compulsion stayed him, brought a question to his mind.

What was the masked killer doing here?

That stalled Jim Strike. It filled him with a vague uneasiness, as if he were about to learn something he did not really wish to know. Everything — the hold-up, the attack by the masked riders, the herd showing up on Tenkiller grazing land and now the presence of the man with the bullet-torn hat, all made no sense — unless Arlie were fully aware of it.

And that he was reluctant to believe.

He watched the *vaquero* stride to the door. He reached unhesitatingly for the knob, twisted it and let himself in. His air of familiarity told Strike that he was no stranger to the house.

Suddenly, things fell into place.

It came to Strike while he stood there, his eyes fastened on the closed door. Angelina was the key. It explained her attitude of coldness toward him. It explained the attempted hold-up and how the *vaquero* knew exactly the amount of money he was supposed to be carrying, the posse that would not listen to reason, that was determined to kill and thus remove all witnesses, and the herd now turning up intact on Tenkiller grazing land.

It all fit. Angelina and the *vaquero* were working hand-in-hand — unknown to Arlie. Otherwise, the masked leader would not have waited until Silvershell had started for town, would not have hidden his horse behind one of the sheds. Likely Francisco Vaca was in on it, too. The Spaniard had trailed him that day with an idea of shooting him in the back but had muffed his chance, very probably. There could be no other answer; Arlie and he were dupes.

A furious anger burst through Jim Strike. He gripped the old shotgun in his hands and started for the house. He moved quietly around the corner of it and halted at the door. Inside he heard the low murmur of the man's laugh. Quite distinctly he heard her ask a question.

"But you are sure he is dead, Pen? There is no doubt?"

"By the saints!" the *vaquero* replied, adding something in Spanish. "He was badly wounded and we know he did not reach the town. He lies somewhere in the forest. My men will find him soon."

"And those he hired?"

"One we left dead at their camp. Another reached the town, died and was buried there by the Shemonite *gringos.* The rest have ridden from the country and will not return."

"I have waited — and wondered."

"You would have known sooner, *muchachita,* except I wanted to be sure of this man, Strike. And your husband was also here. We are too near now to make a mistake and bungle our plan."

Angelina murmured some reply. Then, "The herd?"

"Grazing on the *mesas* west of the valley."

"What did you tell Francisco and the crew?"

"The same as your husband has been told. That I, with some of my riders, were crossing the range and heard shooting. We hurried in to find rustlers attacking this Jim Strike and his crew. We helped drive them away but Strike and two others were killed and the rest, much afraid, ran away. Knowing it was your herd, we then drove it on to your land."

"It is a good story. Arlie believes it. But I am not so sure about Francisco."

"It does not matter," the *vaquero* said. "Francisco is no longer one of us. He has grown a conscience. The day must come when he —"

Strike listened no further. His dark face was pale with a raging fury, his eyes had turned to bits of chilled, gray granite. He shifted the shotgun to his right hand. With the left he reached for the door knob. It turned easily but the panel did not open. It was locked. He fell back a step. He drew up his leg, drove a boot heel against the door. The wooden panel shattered, crashed inward. Strike leaped into the room, shotgun leveled.

The *vaquero* and Angelina were standing in the center of the room. They whirled to face him, springing apart. Surprise and shock and then a sort of fear spread over their features. The man's hand dropped swiftly for the gun at his hip when he recognized Strike. He hesitated as he saw the twin muzzles of the shotgun pointing at his breast.

"Strike!" he exclaimed, "I thought —"

153

"Thought I was dead," Jim finished. "Not quite, but it was close. Who are you, mister?"

The *vaquero*'s lips broke into a faint smile. "Pen Moraga, *señor*. At your service!"

"At yours!" Strike replied in a mocking voice. "And it will be a pleasure to see you hang for the murder of two men!"

He swung his savage, bitter gaze to Angelina. She was beautiful, even in terror. Her green eyes flashed and her features, now pale and transparent, were stilled.

"You'll be hanging right alongside of him," he said, his lips barely moving. "I stood outside and heard the whole story. I expect your next move was to get rid of Arlie. Then the two of you would have had this place all for yourselves."

Angelina had regained her composure. She drew herself up, haughty and confident. "This is the land of my people," she stated proudly. "It has been so since the time of Spain. Now it is mine. I will not share it with any man!"

Pen Moraga turned his head slowly and looked at her. His face was thoughtful.

Strike noted the expression. He laughed. "You didn't expect she was really going to let you be her partner, did you, Moraga? She just used you, same as she's used Arlie and me and anyone else that could do her any good. There's too much greed inside her to ever share anything."

Moraga shrugged. "Two can play such a game."

"Maybe," Strike said, harshly, "but your playing days are done with! You're headed for the end of a rope." He flung a glance at Angelina. She was wearing her robe, only partly dressed. "Get the rest of your clothes on. I'm taking you both in to the law."

"What law?" Angelina asked with a sneer. "There is none in the *gringo* town and the *Commandante* in Paso Largo is a good friend. He will hear only what I tell him."

"There's a deputy marshal in El Paso and a sheriff in Mesilla. I can take you to either one of them."

Angelina flicked him with a scornful glance. "There are many miles to each. You think Pen Moraga is my only friend? There are others. I would need but to call for help."

Strike shook his head. "Still won't work. Besides, Arlie will be along to help. I figure he's going to be plenty interested in things when your friend here starts to talk, trying to save his own neck."

Angelina shrugged disdainfully. "What do I care of Arlie and what he thinks? He is nothing — a clod, a work-horse, a means to an end."

"Be glad to tell him just how you feel." Again the girl moved her slim shoulders. She laughed. "He would not believe you. He will listen only to what I tell him. It is that way with him."

"Could be," Strike murmured. He nodded to Moraga. "All right, take that gun out and drop it on the floor."

The *vaquero* stared at him briefly, shrugged and dropped his hand to the weapon at his hip. His long fingers closed about the white, bone handle.

Strike moved the twin barrels of the shotgun slightly. "You know better than that. Use your left hand."

Moraga allowed his right to fall away. He reached across his waist, grasped the pistol and withdrew it from the holster carefully.

"Drop it."

"You won't reach the *mesa* with him," Angelina promised, her mouth set into a hard line.

"I'll get there — and with both of you," Strike said. "Get on some clothes."

"You think Pen came here alone? You think he does not have his men waiting for him outside?"

"Maybe he does," Strike said, evenly. "And a good way for them to get you both killed is to make a move at stopping me."

Angelina stamped her foot in furious exasperation. She turned suddenly to Moraga. "You fool!" she said in a savage voice. "If you had made certain —"

Moraga swept her rigid shape with a shuttered glance. "It is not finished," he murmured, and flung himself to the floor.

Strike saw him spin over, claw for the pistol lying just beyond his reach. He yelled, "Don't try it!"

Moraga chose to ignore the warning. He caught up the weapon, rolled to his knees. Strike saw the pistol come around, searching for him, heard the crash and whine of lead. The blast of the shotgun shook the house. The charge of lead pellets struck Pen Moraga full in the chest. It lifted him off the floor, slammed him back against the wall, a pulp of torn flesh and smoking cloth.

CHAPTER FOURTEEN

In the swirling cordite smoke, Jim Strike stepped slowly back until his shoulders pressed against the wall behind him. A wave of sickness slogged through him as he looked upon the terrible death the old shotgun had fostered. He lifted his eyes to Angelina. She still stood in the center of the room. She was staring at what once had been Pen Moraga, her perfectly formed lips held to a firm, crimson line, her face empty and pale. There was no horror upon her features, only a revulsion for what she saw.

That fleeting glimpse of her inner self jarred Jim Strike to reality. He came away from the wall in a long step, a towering wildness raging unchecked through him. Angelina saw and darted for the door. He caught her by the wrist, whirled her back into the room. She came up against the bed, fell across it.

"You devil!" he cried. "You ought to be

there on that floor dead instead of that man! You deserve it more than he does! You're a poison — you're like some bad disease that needs stamping out!"

Outside there were sounds of approaching footsteps. The smoke was clearing from the room, drifting slowly toward the splintered doorway and then swiftly pouring outward as it was caught up in some manner of vacuum.

"Niña — niña?" Tia Maria called anxiously from the yard.

Angelina screamed something in a gush of Spanish. The women stopped. Procopio moved cautiously up beside her. Behind them appeared the hostler and the cook, a long meat knife in her hand. They edged uncertainly toward the doorway.

"Get out of here! Get away!" Strike snarled and swung the shotgun in a threatening arc. They hastily withdrew.

Angelina got to her feet. She stood before him, beautiful as graven marble and equally as cold. She studied him for a long minute. Then, "Well, *gringo,* what will you do now? Kill me also?"

Her calmness had a leavening affect upon the boiling anger that had wracked Strike. After a time he said, "Put those clothes on. We're still going to the law."

Angelina smiled at him disdainfully. "Why? Now it is only your word." She stopped, brushed the *vaquero*'s form with a glance. "He does not talk."

"Which doesn't change anything, far as I'm concerned," Strike replied. "You still planned out the whole thing and I have other ways of proving it. You never did intend for Arlie and me to own this ranch, did you? From the start, it was just a way to get this place rebuilt for your own purpose."

Angelina's eyes flared. "You think I would let him or anybody else have my land? It has been the place of my people for three hundred years — the *Hacienda de Mondragon!* It shall always be!

"And some day it shall be as it was in the old days. The *peons* will work the land and the *ricos* again shall enjoy the ways of the *aristocracias!*"

"With you as the queen of it all," Strike finished, sarcasm sharpening his voice. "But you overshot the mark this time."

Angelina shook her head. "There is no one to believe you, Jim Strike."

"I'll worry about that."

"You are thinking of Arlie. He will believe what I wish him to believe." Strike said, "Maybe. Get dressed. We're leaving here." Angelina did not move. "You are a great fool, Jim," she said in a normal, rational voice. "Arlie is your friend but you know nothing of him. And in the days you have been here, you have learned nothing. He will believe only what I say, he will think only the thoughts I wish him to think. He is a child in my hands."

"We'll wait and see," Strike said. "You've changed him, I'll admit that. You have all but destroyed him, but I think the day of reckoning has come. He will listen to the truth now."

Angelina glanced beyond him, through the open doorway. "Your chance will soon come," she said, her face wicked with its secret smile. "He is here. Now we shall see who is the stronger, the wife or the friend."

Strike heard the sudden rush of a horse in the yard. Arlie's voice sang out, high-pitched with worry.

"What's wrong here? Heard a gunshot." Tia Maria and Procopio both replied in a chorus of jumbled words. Arlie started for the house at a fast run.

Angelina swung her eyes to Strike. She smiled, *Adios gringo,* she murmured. "We could have been good friends if you would have had it so. Now you will be dead."

She lifted her hands, seized the hems of her robe and ripped them apart, tearing

161

away the buttons and the edges of the cloth. She shook her head violently, spilling the golden folds of her hair about her shoulders into a wild disarray. She waited another moment until the bulking shadow of her husband blocked the doorway and then screamed.

"Arlie!" she sobbed and threw herself at him.

Silvershell gathered her into his thick arms, held her close. He soothed her with gentle words and strokes of his broad hands. He looked over her shoulder at Strike, his face set and slowly beginning to flush.

"What's been going on around here?" he demanded. "Heard you were dead, shot down by rustlers." He stopped, his gaze halting upon the shapeless form of the *vaquero.* "Who's that?"

Strike said, "Name's Pen Moraga. He was the leader of the bunch who tried to hold me up —"

"Moraga!" Arlie echoed. He took Angelina by the shoulders, held her at arm's length and searched her face. "Your cousin?"

Angelina nodded, her wracking sobs filling the room.

"He headed up that bunch of so-called rustlers and killed two of my crew. Would have finished me off, too, if I hadn't made it to town. That yarn he told you was all lies — and it was all cooked up by him and your wife, there, to get everything for themselves. From the start —"

"What was that?" Silvershell broke in sharply, his big head snapping up.

"Don't believe him, Arlie!" Angelina cried. "Don't believe anything he says! He's just trying to come between us, break us apart. He wants me to leave with him!"

Arlie Silvershell's face faded into a stiff, white mask. He pushed the girl to one side, looked at her closely. He apparently had, at that moment, noticed the ripped and torn condition of her robe. He came slowly about to Strike, his huge shape squared away. There was disbelief in his eyes; disbelief and a burning suspicion.

Strike said, "There's no truth in that, Arlie. She's been making suckers out of both of us. Out of plenty other men too, it seems. There must be half a dozen more —"

"He hates me!" Angelina wailed. "He always has and I never did anything to him. I wanted to be his friend, for your sake, but he wouldn't have it that way. He said it had to be just the two of us — or nothing!"

"It's not true —" Strike insisted.

"He came here this morning, waited until after you were gone," Angelina continued, clinging to Silvershell. "I tried to make him go away but he wouldn't. I locked the door to keep him out — but he kicked it and came in anyway."

Silvershell glanced at the shattered door, his face beginning to work spasmodically. His eyes were glowing with an insane sort of anger. "My own friend — my best friend —"

"That's a lie, Arlie," Strike broke in, striving to keep his voice calm. "It wasn't the way she claims."

"He got inside and then poor Pen happened to come. He wanted to see you, he said. He heard me screaming while I tried to fight Jim off. He came in to stop him but Jim was like a wild man — a terrible wild man!"

Strike stood as a man transfixed, appalled by the parade of outrageous lies. He had expected something of this sort but nothing so fantastic. His own anger began to lift with succeeding moments.

"Arlie — for your own sake, listen to me!"

"It was terrible!" Angelina moaned. "I kept fighting him off, but he is so strong! And then Pen and he started to fight. He shot down Pen, killed him with that gun he is holding. Murdered him when he tried to protect me."

Silvershell stared across the width of the small room, his eyes now glowing with rage and hatred. His hand slid to the pistol at his side.

"I'm going to kill you, Jim —"

"Don't touch that gun!" Strike snapped. He brought the shotgun up in a sudden blur of motion. "I don't want to use this, Arlie, but if I have to, I will!"

Silvershell paused. He did not remove his glittering gaze from Strike. The room was hushed, even Angelina's wrenching sobs ceased.

"You're going to listen to me," Strike said, "even at gunpoint. You've got to know what this woman is doing to you."

"Save your wind," Silvershell replied in a dead, cold voice. "Should have known five years would change a man, twist him around."

"You've got to believe what I'm telling you," Strike went on. "I stood outside this room and heard her and this Pen Moraga talking. They were building the ranch up for themselves. She didn't intend to ever share it with you and me. She only wanted what we could do for her in making it what it used to be years ago.

"That's why Moraga and his bunch tried to rob me. She's the one who told them how much money I would be carrying. They were partners in the whole scheme. If they could have gotten their hands on the money, then I would have been out of the partnership. Moraga failed and they had to think of something else."

Silvershell wagged his head back and forth. He accepted none of it. "Reckon I can believe my own eyes."

Strike said, "I admit breaking in that door. I had to. They were inside and they had it locked. I was after Moraga for killing two of my crew. I was taking them both to the sheriff."

Silvershell said, "Even if I believed that, it wouldn't make no sense. Moraga was Angelina's cousin. What's wrong with a woman talking to her cousin?"

"Cousin!" Strike echoed. "Didn't sound that way to me."

"Proves one thing to me," Arlie said. "You told so many lies you got yourself tangled up in them."

"You don't want to take my word, maybe I can find somebody that can prove what I'm telling you is the truth. There are a few men in Paso Largo that might be made to talk. And maybe your own ranch hands could tell you a few things that would surprise you."

Silvershell's eyes narrowed. "Who would you be meaning?"

"Any of them, if they would talk."

Arlie shook his head. "No good. I don't figure I'd believe them anyway because you probably have set it up with them. I caught you, right in this room with Angelina. You even say you kicked in the door. That's proof enough for me that she's telling the truth."

His hand drifted again to the pistol at his hip. Behind him Angelina's voice suddenly shrilled: "Kill him, Arlie! Kill him! Kill him for what he did to me!"

Strike brought back the hammers of the shotgun, the noise a loud clacking in the room. Silvershell froze.

"Don't try anything, Arlie," Strike said, his voice almost pleading. "Don't make me use this. She's not worth it — believe that! Just stand where you are."

He eased closer to Silvershell, circled around the big Missourian warily. He reached out, pulled the pistol from its oiled holster. With a quick flip of his wrist he sent it spinning out into the yard.

"Now step back. I'm going outside and get on my horse. Don't try to follow."

"I'll kill you," Arlie promised in a thick, flat voice. "I'll hunt you down, Strike, wherever you go. You can't get away from me."

"Don't follow me," Strike repeated. "Be hell for a man to kill his best friend. Don't force me to do it."

He moved toward the doorway, never taking his eyes off Silvershell. Behind the yellow-haired man's half-crouched shape he could see Angelina. She was watching with a sly amusement, her green eyes wicked in victory. He didn't want to kill Arlie Silvershell. He in no way feared the man; in any clash he was confident he was by far the faster with a pistol or a shotgun. The result could only end in death for Arlie. The difference of their ways of life during those past five years was the gaugestick; Arlie worked in a mine, he had worked with a gun.

He reached the opening, prepared to take a careful, backward step that would place him outside. He must get away from the ranch, avoid more trouble if at all possible. If he could make Long Pass, or Paso Largo and get out of sight . . . His foot felt the solid surface of the earth and he shifted his weight to it.

An object came hurtling across the room.

Angelina had thrown something, a pillow or a folded bit of clothing. It struck the shotgun, knocked it aside. In that fragment of time he saw Arlie Silvershell lunge.

CHAPTER FIFTEEN

Silvershell's lowered shoulder caught Strike mid-center. Strike threw the shotgun aside, fearing it would discharge from the impact and send a murderous blast of lead ripping into his friend's body. He staggered backwards, threw his arm about Arlie to prevent himself from falling. He was off balance and he went down, Arlie on top.

He struck the ground with a solidness that smashed the wind from his lungs. But he kept his presence of mind. He drew his knees up fast, hard. Arlie groaned as pain shot through his groin. He rolled to one side, struck out feebly at Jim's face. Strike jerked away and the blow skidded off his cheek bone, roughing the skin raw.

He felt Silvershell's fingers claw at his throat, clamp down upon it. He began to choke. Again he brought up his knees and Arlie cursed and twisted away. It was all Strike needed. He jammed his hands into

Silvershell's armpits, heaved upward. In the same instant he rolled from under the man's crushing weight. Silvershell went over like a huge log, into the dust.

Strike was up instantly. Silvershell was no more than a breath behind him. Strike circled the poised, heaving man warily, arms outstretched, fingers splayed, head hung forward.

"Arlie — listen to me?" he tried again. "Hear me out! I'll prove what I'm telling you!"

"I'll kill you!" Silvershell roared and lunged.

Strike faded from his clutch, stepped nimbly aside. He drove a light blow to Silvershell's ribs as he rocked by. It was an ineffectual punch but it served its purpose. Arlie, knocked off stride, tripped and dropped to hands and knees.

"Listen to me, Arlie —" Silvershell yelled something unintelligible. He sprang to his feet, whirled. The man was insanely angry, goaded by a wild, unreasonable jealousy and a raging fury.

"If it's the last thing I do — I'll kill you!"

Strike realized in that moment it was a hopeless cause. There was no talking to the man while he was in such a frame of mind. It was senseless to try further. Arlie was like a crazed steer, blind to everything, wanting only to injure and maim. He would get this over with quick and leave, as he had started to do, hoping Arlie would cool off and become reasonable later.

He braced himself for a charge. The murderous fury was warping Silvershell's judgement, hurrying greatly but penalizing the wisdom of his movements. He was easy to avoid. He stepped in. Strike again moved lightly away. In the next instant a shower of lights burst brilliantly inside his head. He felt himself going over backwards, his legs unexpectedly giving out beneath him.

He struck the ground flat, dust spurting out from under him. He was not hurt so much as surprised. Arlie had neatly out-guessed him, tricked him. He should have known better. Arlie was an old hand at rough and tumble; Strike had seen him in action many times during their army days. He grinned at his own error, rolled quickly aside to avoid Arlie's swinging boot, bounded to his feet.

He spun away, moving in a short, tight circle. Arlie halted, flat-footed and suddenly uncertain. Strike moved in from the right, stunned the man with a left that jolted the Missourian to his heels. He followed with an iron-hard right that began somewhere behind him and traveled the full distance. It caught the wavering Arlie directly on the point of his jaw. Silvershell seemed to lift inches off the ground and went over in a stiffening heap.

Strike threw a hasty glance at him. He was out, there was little doubt of that and should remain so for several minutes. Strike wheeled about, scooped up Silvershell's pistol and thrust it into his own holster. He looked toward the house. Angelina was standing in the doorway viewing it all with calm interest. When she saw Strike retrieve Arlie's weapon, she straightened perceptibly but she did not retreat into the safety of the room. She watched him with cool eyes.

Jim Strike had no thought of putting a bullet into her lovely body, no matter how much she deserved it. He had one thing in mind; get away from Arlie, get as far as possible from him before the fight resolved itself into a question of life or death between them. Once the wild, blinding anger was gone, perhaps he would listen.

He turned and started for the pole corral at a run. Angelina screamed something in Spanish. Procopio materialized from a side door of the house near the kitchen. He carried an ancient musket in his bony arms. Strike drew his pistol — Arlie's — and snapped a hasty shot into the dust a yard ahead of the old Mexican. Procopio hauled up short, dropped the gun. It exploded with a roar, sending its ball off toward the canyon. The man turned and fled back into the house.

The bay was standing at the corral, a dozen yards distant. At that moment the hostler emerged from the barn carrying a hayfork. He saw Strike racing toward him, gun still in hand. He whirled and ducked back into the gloomy depths of the building. Strike reached the bay. He yanked the reins free and flung himself onto the saddle. He wheeled about, took the trail that led across the rear of the ranch. As he thundered out of the yard he glanced to where Arlie had fallen. The man was sitting up, rubbing dazedly at his jaw. Angelina, a pistol in her hand, was urging him to accept the weapon, to get up.

Strike wasted no more time in looking. He put the gelding into a fast, long-reaching gallop, threading his way between the corrals and outbuildings, rushing for the smooth road that lay beyond. He reached the last of the structures and came to the fork. To his right lay the narrow, steep trail which led to the flats above, the left joined the main road that wound down the floor of the valley on and out between the buttes.

He swung the bay unhesitatingly towards the valley road. The trail would have been a good idea if he had had a better start on Silvershell. He could have then reached the flats quickly and wheeled off into the hollows and down behind the ridges and soon lost himself. But he had too little time; Arlie, at Angelina's insistence, would be close on him and, since taking the ravine trail to the flats would necessitate the bay's moving slowly, he would present an easy target for even the poorest marksman.

He reached the main road and raced along the edge of the pond, the bay's hoofs fairly flying. They rounded the end of the water, lengthened out on the smooth straightaway. The gelding was enjoying each moment of the mad flight but Strike knew he would have to pull him down to a slower pace soon. It was a long ride to the town and he would need some of that strength later on.

He risked a glance over his shoulder. He was startled to see Arlie so close. Astride his big, red sorrel, he was halfway around the pond, bent low in the saddle, coming like a wind from the north.

Strike swore softly. Why couldn't Arlie have been another minute getting to his feet and taking up the pursuit! He was going to force them into a showdown yet — which was what Angelina wanted, Strike realized in that next instant. He looked ahead. He could see no suitable place where he might swing off and hide. It was going to be up to the bay and he had his work cut out for him trying to outrun the long-legged sorrel. The way Silvershell felt he likely would run the red horse into the ground if necessary.

He looked back again. Arlie and the sorrel had completed the curcuit of the pond, were now directly behind and coming up fast. The faint, flat echo of a gunshot reached Strike. Arlie had his pistol up and was firing. The distance was too far and there was no danger from the bullets, but it gave Strike an even better insight as to Silvershell's determination.

He crouched lower over the gelding's bulging neck, called upon him for greater speed. The bay responded, his long legs seeming to stretch out beneath him until they were almost horizontal with his belly while the road rushed by below them in a brown and green blur. Strike chanced another look at Silvershell. He had not gained; indeed, it appeared that he had dropped back a few yards. But the bay could not maintain such a pace for long. It was much too fast.

Strike turned his attention to the country ahead. They were approaching the mouth of the valley. He could see the frowning face of the west butte, standing out sharp and clear in the morning sunlight. He tried to recall the country surrounding that portion of the valley, hoping to remember some place, some area that would enable him to duck from sight, throw Silvershell off his trail and allow him to eventually lose the man. He could think of none.

Arlie and the sorrel began to close the gap again. The bay, while fast as most horses of his size and type, was inclined to a slower, steadier pace that would cover more ground in a day's time. And Silvershell was pressing the big red mercilessly, determined to catch up and even the score at any price. Strike heard the sharp crack of Silvershell's gun again. There was no warning whine of a bullet. He was still beyond range.

They drew abreast the buttes and broke out onto the open plains country. A long, shallow wash curved off to the left and Strike, still hoping to delay Silvershell in some way, pointed the bay into it. The path was gently downgrade and the bay rushed on ahead without slackening his speed. They quickly reached the floor. Strike threw a glance back toward the buttes. Silvershell was not yet in sight.

If they could cover another hundred yards, they would reach a sharp turn in the wash and might be hidden there for a brief time; enough, at least, to cause Arlie to slow down and search the landscape for signs of the man he pursued.

The bay was beginning to blow when they reached the end. Strike allowed him to pull down. He looked again toward the rim. Arlie was still not there. Strike took a deep breath. Now, if the bay could have only a few minutes rest and still maintain the lead he had, Strike would be willing to match him against the long-legged sorrel without fear for the balance of the distance to Long Pass.

But Jim Strike had not reckoned with the keen knowledge Arlie Silvershell had of the Tenkiller country. Strike allowed the bay to loaf along easily until the wash spent itself and ran out onto a flat expanse of open *mesa.* As they emerged, he half turned, expecting to see the big Missourian halted on the rim searching the plains for him.

What he saw was Silvershell less than a hundred yards distant. He was coming off the brow of a low hill, the sorrel running fast and easy, tail and mane streaming out in the breeze. Arlie, knowing the land, had continued straight on when Strike had dropped from view. He had wasted no time in looking about, knowing Strike would eventually have to come out onto the flats somewhere ahead.

Strike drove spurs into the bay, sending him forward in a startled burst of speed. In the same instant Silvershell began to shoot. Strike heard the whine of bullets now, dangerously close. He dragged his own pistol from its holster. The moments were becoming desperate and he prepared to fight for his life if it came down to that.

He twisted about, intending to throw several quick shots ahead of the sorrel, kick dust up into the big red's nostrils in the hope of slowing him down. He fired once, saw Silvershell duck lower over his saddle at the sound of the report. Arlie snapped a shot at him. Strike immediately felt the burn of a bullet as it streaked across his right thigh. He glanced down quickly. Blood already was oozing from the long, shallow furrow.

The bullet had almost unseated him. The bay swerved widely from the trail at his sudden knee pressure and drag at the reins. Strike hurriedly brought him back into the wagon-wheel tracks but it had cost them precious footage. Strike's jaw hardened.

That last bullet had been close, too close. It appeared he could not escape Arlie, that he would be compelled to have it out with him unless he wanted to get shot off his horse.

He moved forward in the saddle, making it easier to turn more completely around and take a better aim at the man behind him. He brought up his gun, lowered it. Arlie was no longer there. He saw the sorrel then, and next, Arlie. They were off to the left of the road. The red horse was struggling to his feet, shaking himself free of dust that bulged about him in a thin cloud. Not far from him, Silvershell was down on his hands and knees. The sorrel had stumbled and gone down.

Strike slowed the gelding, watched Silvershell closely. Neither man nor horse seemed to be hurt. At least the sorrel was walking slowly about in a circle. Strike held the bay to a steady pace and watched Arlie. The Missourian was up, moving about, testing his legs and arms, shaking his head as if to clear it.

The bay topped out a long slope, dropped over to the opposite side traveling easily and with no amount of effort. Strike, with his bandana, had checked the flow of blood coming from his wound. He had been lucky a second time, for it was little more than a scratch. He looked back. Arlie was not in view. He was either still below the ridge or else he had given up the chase and turned back.

It was near noon and the heat was beginning to make itself felt. He took a drink from his canteen. They were not far from Long Pass, now. The bay, sweated to froth, would have no trouble making it unless, of course, he was pressed into another hard run. Thinking of that possibility reminded Strike of Silvershell. He raised himself in the stirrups, twisted and threw a glance to his back trail.

Arlie was still coming.

CHAPTER SIXTEEN

The hours wore slowly on, marked by the increasing heat and a gradual stiffening of his leg. The wound was minor and it no longer bled, but the stiffness worried him. It was bound to make him slow and awkward on his feet and that, should it come to a showdown with Arlie, he could not afford. He now sat slightly to one side of the saddle, his left leg bent at the knee to permit the right, injured member to hang rigidly outward.

Long Pass came into view when he topped the next crest. He glanced back over the trail. Arlie Silvershell was a high shape on the sorrel three-quarters of a mile back, coming on like a patient, unshakable shadow. Strike rode off the hill and down into the settlement, coming in at the far end of its main street. The bay, sensing the end of the journey, pricked up his ears and quickened his step as he headed toward

Hannah Moore's place.

But he could not go to Hannah Moore.

Strike realized that the moment his eyes fell upon her doorway. He could not seek aid from her. Long Pass was not so large that Arlie would not quickly find him and in the ensuing trouble, Hannah might get hurt. He simply would not risk that; he would take no chances on her becoming involved in any manner. He pulled the bay sharply back into the street, wishing then he had taken a different route, one that would have kept his arrival a secret. He held his gaze straight ahead. If he were lucky, she would be in the rear of her establishment and would not see him pass.

He considered his next move. He could stop at the hotel, but that offered no real solution since Arlie would quickly locate him there. And the reason for his long flight from the ranch had been to place himself beyond Silvershell's ranch; keep away from him until he had simmered down and had a chance to come to his senses. What point in halting now and allowing Arlie to find him?

Across the border, in Paso Largo, lay the answer. He knew that at once. There were dozens of places where a man could go and drop from sight for a few days; and people in Paso Largo did not answer questions, especially those asked by a stranger such as Arlie would be. Perhaps there would be a doctor available, too, where he could get his leg treated. He might even get off a letter to that lawman at Mesilla or El Paso and bring him into the matter. Perhaps the presence of the law might more quickly bring Arlie around.

Jim Strike stirred restlessly in his saddle. He was impatient with the position he found himself in. Never before had he backed down from any man! And now he was even considering the advisability of bringing in the law to protect himself! A hell of a note. The idea galled, like sweat on a raw saddle sore. But he had little choice. Arlie Silvershell was his friend, despite the way the yellow-haired Missourian felt toward him at the moment. He could not — would not — fight him with a gun.

He rode slowly down the street, nodding to the store-keeper where he had bought supplies that day before he and his crew had ridden out for Galesburg. It seemed a long time gone and, thinking of it, he recalled the letter he had written to Aaron Hendrix's wife. She and her sons should have arrived by now. He wondered how she felt when told her husband was dead. He wished he had been around to tell her. It was his place. As soon as things settled down he would look her up, talk to her and make some sort of arrangements for her and her two sons.

He reached the end of the street and followed out the dusty road which led across the border. He touched the bay with spurs, changing the pace from a walk to a slow gallop. The movement echoed pain through his leg but it was not bad. As soon as it had been bathed and dressed it would be all right. The skin felt stiff and drawn now. Hot water and medicine would relieve that.

He wanted to reach Paso Largo well ahead of Arlie. He needed to look around, get his bearings and find a good place in which to hole up. He turned to see if Arlie was in sight. He was, doggedly following a short mile away.

Strike rode down the center of the border town's main street. There were few persons abroad at this hot hour of the day and those who were stared briefly at the blood-stained bandage about his leg and passed on. Such things were common in Paso Largo. Men came and went with their troubles and no one bothered to inquire about them.

He located the saloon where he had stood at the bar and hired on a crew. It seemed the best bet since the bartender there was an American and possibly would remember him. He circled to the rear of the building, to the horse barn. He pulled up just inside the wide, double doors and dismounted, stiff and slow of movement.

The hostler emerged from a tack room and watched him in silence. He stepped forward and accepted the reins from Strike with a faint nod. He was Mexican and apparently spoke no English — and most likely understood none, either. But talk was unnecessary. One look at the sweaty, dust-crusted bay horse conveyed Strike's wishes. He grinned as he accepted a coin from Strike and led the gelding back into the murky depths of the building.

Strike turned and made his way to the back of the saloon. He walked with considerable difficulty, the pressure of his weight upon the injured leg breaking open the wound and making it bleed again. He did not bother to adjust the makeshift bandage and try to stop the flow. There was not time for that. He reached the rear stairs to the saloon, climbed the half-dozen steps with awkward, halting labor and entered the structure. As before, there were only a few customers.

It was a different bartender. Strike leaned against the counter, ordered a whiskey. He downed it and poured himself another from the bottle.

"Saw a deputy marshal around here a few days ago. He still around?"

The bartender paused in his glass polishing, looked closely at Jim. After a time he shrugged. "None. Rode out two, three days back." He again peered at Strike. "You lookin' for some law?"

Strike shook his head. "Just a thought. Where can a man get a room around here where he won't be bothered for a spell?"

The bartender studied him for a third time, now reading some sort of meaning of his own into the inquiries and connecting them to the stained bandage about Strike's leg. He said, "Was I wantin' to stay out of sight, I'd go to Amy's place. Right across the street."

Strike glanced through the doorway to the curtained windows of the house on the opposite side of the dusty strip. The bartender saw the question in his eyes.

"Oh, the girls'll leave you be, you tell Amy you want it so."

Strike finished his drink, nodded. He laid a coin on the counter. "Obliged if you forget you've ever seen me," he murmured and started across the wide room. Amy's place sounded like the answer to his needs. He doubted if Arlie would look for him there.

A tall figure rose from one of the tables as he passed. He saw the man from the corner of his eye. Chris Calloway. He came to a slow halt. He wanted no trouble now, no delay. Arlie would be drawing near. But he was too angry to avoid it. Running from Silvershell was one thing, from another man was something else. He wheeled about, favoring the injured leg unconsciously.

"Something on your mind?"

Calloway stared at him for a moment. His eyes lowered to the bandage, came back up. The tenseness faded from his features. He said, "Some other time," and sat down.

"Don't let this leg bother you," Strike said. "You got some notions, let's hear them."

Calloway shook his head. "Some other time, friend."

Strike shrugged and pushed out through the scarred batwings onto the gallery. He looked down the street. Arlie and the sorrel were just breaking into view. Strike sighed and walked out into the brilliant sunshine, headed for the closed doors of Amy's place. Maybe one of the girls would be handy with a bullet wound. He hoped so. He was growing a bit tired of favoring the leg and it was too late to run down to a doctor.

Hannah Moore had been standing at the window of her small establishment watching several children at play when she saw Jim Strike ride into view. Her heart had leaped at sight of his broad-shouldered form and an overflowing gladness filled her. He had completed the chore he had set forth for himself and now he was returning to her. It was much sooner than she had expected. Had something gone wrong?

She watched his approach and when the bay began to angle toward her, she turned swiftly and hurried to the kitchen. She placed the coffee pot on the stove, poked at the fire to start a blaze. This done, she started back for the door, pausing only seconds to critically examine herself in a wall mirror and brush a stray lock of hair into place.

She reached the doorway, prepared to greet him, but there she halted in surprise and disappointment. Jim hadn't stopped. She looked out onto the street and had a glimpse of him a dozen yards away, continuing on down into the town. Then she saw the bloody bandage about his leg and turned to rush out, to call him and bring him back. But something stayed the impulse. There was some good reason why he had not come to her. She had seen him

189

heading for her place, but some second thought had altered his purpose.

Why hadn't he stopped?

He had been hurt and should have come to her, turned to her in his moment of need and allowed her to look after him. He could not have changed in his feeling for her so quickly, she was certain. And if he had, Jim Strike was not the kind to just brush her away, ignore her. He would come to her and tell her. No, he had other reasons; either he did not feel he should trouble her or he had wanted to spare her some sort of danger. Oh, men were such fools! They never seemed to realize a woman wanted just that sort of need! That they thrived on being of help to those they loved?

She saw Arlie Silvershell at that moment.

He came riding down the center of the street on a big, red sorrel. The horse was near spent, his steps lagging and unsteady. Arlie's face was a grim, tight mask, his eyes fierce, burning pots of hatred. He had a cocked pistol in his hand as though he expected to make use of it at any instant. Her one glimpse of the distraught man told her the story.

There had been trouble of some kind at the ranch, Jim had been shot and now his partner, Arlie — it must be Arlie since it fitted the description Jim had given her — was after him, seeking to kill him. Jim was trying to keep out of the man's way, unwilling to fight. She doubted if it was because Jim feared to face Silvershell. He was running away because he loved the tall, yellow-haired man as a brother and simply refused to shoot it out with him.

She understood then why Jim had changed his mind and not stopped when he reached town. He had been thinking of her, afraid she might get hurt, that he might draw her into his troubles. He had gone across into Paso Largo where he could hide out.

But he needed her — and his troubles were her troubles as well. She turned quickly, snatched her stiffly starched bonnet from its peg and drew it on. She was going to him whether he thought it wise or not.

She came out into the streaming noonday sunlight: Silvershell was at the far end of the street, just turning onto the border-town road. She started for the livery stable behind the hotel, walking fast. She reached it breathless from her efforts. The hostler came out to greet her, a wondering frown on his face.

"Yes'm, Mrs. Moore?"

"I need a horse and buggy, Mr. Chard. Quickly."

CHAPTER SEVENTEEN

Jim Strike stretched out on the old iron-poster bedstead and stared at the ceiling. Amy had given him a front room, one that overlooked the street, as he had requested. She, herself, had dressed his wound, cauterizing it with raw whiskey and bandaging it for him. She had promised he would not be disturbed and that anyone, making inquiry for him, would be turned aside.

Now he was safely out of the way. Let Arlie search the town over. He would never think to look in a house such as Amy ran and if by chance he did, Amy would send him packing. By dark Arlie should have calmed down enough, anyway, to listen to reason. If not, Strike was prepared to stay under cover for longer, if need be.

Arlie was out there on the street now. A few minutes earlier, Strike had risen to open one of the two windows that fronted the building. The room was stuffy from heat and a sickly, sweet perfume. The outside air was hot but at least it was fresh, tainted only by dust. He had noted the sorrel then, standing worn and hipshot before a saloon a hundred yards away. Arlie evidently was systematically checking the town, building by building. That should take considerable time. There were a great number of saloons in Paso Largo.

But suppose Arlie, tipped off by someone who had seen Strike enter Amy's, did find him?

He lay flat on his back and stared at the grimy ceiling. The war was a long time back but a man doesn't soon forget the good things that came out of it even after five years have passed. You just don't kill your best friend, the man who saved your life under fire and made it possible for you to be alive and breathing at that very moment.

But did you owe him your life in the sense that you should stand by and allow him to take it?

That made no sense. There was no debt so large that it could be paid only by the creditor being permitted to kill the debtor. A man might sacrifice his own life to save that of the one who, as Arlie had done, prevented certain death at another time. That was natural and even to be expected.

Repayment by giving your life to save that of your benefactor. But to stand by and allow oneself to be shot down — that could not be expected of any man.

And if Arlie found him?

Then it would be Arlie or him. There could be no other answer. He would regret it all the rest of his days if he were forced to shoot down his best friend. But if it had to be that way, then so be it. He would know he had done his best to avoid a fatal collision between them. Arlie would be thrusting the fight upon him, against his wishes. He could always remember that when his conscience began to plague him. But there would be small solace in that. His one great hope was that Arlie would not find him; that no showdown between them would ever come.

He wished he had been able to talk to Hannah, even if for only a minute. She would be wondering what had taken place at the ranch, worrying if he was all right or not. He might have let her know, told her that he would see her shortly; that as soon as the problem with Arlie was straightened out, he wanted her for his wife.

But he was glad he had waited. He did not fear to face Arlie, but things can happen to a man. Small accidents that throw him off, deter his speed and slow down his reflexes. Nothing is ever certain, he well knew. It was better to wait and talk of marriage to Hannah after he had his personal problems cleared up.

He became aware of a pounding on the door below. It was loud and insistent. He lay quietly, listening for several moments and then suddenly aroused and suspicious, he came off the bed in a single bound. Pain shot through him in a jagged thunderbolt when his injured leg felt the weight of his body. He ignored it, hurried to the window and looked down into the street.

He could not see the front entrance to Amy's establishment. It was directly below his quarters and the roof of the building's small gallery cut it off from view. The knocking had ceased, anyway, and whoever it had been apparently had gone on his way. Strike turned about and limped back to his bed. He stretched out once more, grateful for the comfort.

And then Arlie Silvershell was standing before him.

He had mounted the stairway, walked the length of the hall unheard. He had opened the door to Strike's room quietly. He now stood framed in that opening, his huge, threatening shape almost filling it. He wore no hat, his clothing was dusty and sweat-stained. His broad face was set into grim lines and his eyes glowed with a maniacal light.

"You'll never find a hole deep enough to hide from me!" he said in a tight, suppressed way.

Jim Strike raised himself slowly to a sitting position on the bed. A pistol was in Arlie's hand, the hammer already back, ready for firing. His own weapon was in its holster hanging by the belt from the bedpost. It was well beyond his reach. He watched the Missourian's flushed face, riding out the terrible moments.

He said, "Understand this, Arlie. I'm up here for one reason. Not because I'm afraid of you, but because I don't want trouble with you."

"You've got it, whether you want it or not," Silvershell replied. "I'm going to kill you, Jim. No man does to me what you did, friend or not."

Strike shook his head. "You're all wrong. None of what you're thinking is true. And maybe I can prove it if you will give me the chance. There's a cowboy across the street, in the saloon. Name of Calloway. He was in on that hold-up and I've got a hunch he knows plenty about a lot of other things. If we can make him talk —"

"Calloway? Blond-headed fellow?"

Strike said, "That's him. Was sitting at a corner table when I came through."

Silvershell granted. "Met him. He's the one who told me where you was hiding. He don't know nothing. Fact is, he's probably gone. Said he was riding out today."

"Riding out!" Strike repeated, his hopes sagging at the words. "That ought to prove something to you. He's afraid we'll pin him down!"

Arlie shook his head angrily. "I ain't here to listen to a lot more argument from you! I've heard all the talk I'm going to!"

Strike watched him lift the pistol, level it. One fact was suddenly clear to him; it was useless to try and reason with Arlie. This was the end of the road.

"Reach out there and get your gun," Silvershell ordered. "I ain't ever shot an unarmed man. I won't start now, not even with you."

Strike shook his head. "I won't draw against you, Arlie."

Silvershell swore. He took a step forward, yanked Strike's weapon from its holster. With a quick flip of his wrist he tossed it. Strike caught the heavy pistol with his right hand.

"Now you're armed. If you won't use that gun, it's your own damned fault."

Jim Strike's broad shoulders went down as despair settled over him. There was no relenting in Silvershell. He would listen to nothing, he would have his satisfaction.

"On your feet!" Arlie snapped. "And keep that gun hanging at your side. You make a sudden move and I won't wait!"

In the tense, hot quiet of the stuffy room, Jim Strike pivoted about. He placed his feet on the floor. He rose slowly. Taking a long breath he turned to face Arlie.

Silvershell was watching him with a close intentness, alert for some sort of trick. He lowered his own gun to his side, allowing it to hang, as did Strike's.

"I'll count to three —" he said and suddenly stopped.

Strike saw his brows come down in a frown. There was a dark shadow behind the big man, almost hidden by his bulk; someone standing in the hallway just outside the door. Silvershell's arm came up gradually.

The voice of Francisco Vaca, calm and faintly accented said, "Step inside the room, *señor.*"

Arlie Silvershell complied. Vaca, keeping the barrel of his gun pressed into the Missourian's back, reached up and took the weapon from the big man's fingers. He tossed it onto the bed. He glanced at Strike, his meaning plain. Strike laid his pistol alongside it.

"What's this all about, Francisco?" Arlie demanded, his voice quivering with rage. "You in with this —"

The Spaniard leaned back against the door frame. He shook his head. "I cannot let you do this. Already there has been too much blood wasted."

"You stay out of this —" Arlie began, but Vaca waved him to silence.

"What your friend has told you is true, *señor*. This I know, for I was part of it. But I did not bargain for so much death."

Silvershell's face had become a mask. He stared at Vaca. "What are you talking about? What do you know about it?"

"Tia Maria told me of the happenings at the ranch this morning. I rode at once, hoping to come in time. This man is your friend, *señor*. Your only friend, perhaps. The things he has told you are true."

"About my wife?" Arlie asked in a strangled voice.

Vaca said, "Your wife is a strong woman and a most proud one. She would have the *hacienda* as it was in the old days and there are those who agree. I, among them. My father and my father's father, and those before him, served the Mondragons, and always it has been a position of honor.

"But with the new *señora* it is an unholy thing. It is lies and lust and death. And friend against friend. It was so from the start, from the day of your marriage. You were to be the husband until the *hacienda* was rebuilt. Then there was to come an accident. It was ordered so. And there was death for your friend, also. I followed him onto the *mesa* that first day to tell him so, but my courage failed."

"But I found him — Strike, with my wife. Just like she said —"

"The words were not truth, *señor.* Moraga was there, as your friend has said. It was to be marriage between them when all things were ready."

"Marriage!" Silvershell echoed. "They were cousins!"

Francisco Vaca shook his head slowly. "Not cousins, lovers. They told you, and others, such a lie, that they could be often together."

In the stifling silence Jim Strike raised his glance to meet that of his friend. Arlie was staring at him, his eyes filled with humiliation and shame. A wave of pity swept through Strike.

"There is still time," Vaca said, his clipped, stilted words breaking the quiet. "You are the husband of the *señor* and with firm hand you will change her thoughts. You will make her see —"

"No!" Arlie Silvershell shouted and snatched up his gun from the bed. "I'll kill her!"

He whirled to the doorway. Francisco Vaca moved in to block him. Arlie struck out, a long, swinging back-handed blow. It caught the Spaniard across the face, slammed him back against the wall. He settled to the floor soundlessly.

"Arlie!" Strike yelled. But the big man's shape was already at the end of the hallway.

Strike knelt beside Vaca, examined him briefly. He was knocked out but unhurt. Strike moved back to the bed. He siezed his clothing and began to finish his dressing, working in feverish haste. He heard a shout outside, down in the street. He wheeled to the window, looked. Arlie, either because of his sorrel's fagged condition or because the horse was several hundred yards down the street, had chosen not to ride him. He had swung onto a husky little buckskin, was pounding for the road. A shout of protest went up behind him. He did not slow.

Strike leaped across the room, forgetful of

his injured leg. He buckled on his gun belt as he ran along the hall, turned at the landing and hammered down the short stairway. Amy's square, rouged face peered at him from a partly opened door as he came along the lower passage. She started to voice a question but he rushed on by.

Arlie must be stopped. He had gone completely berserk. He would not let up now until he had taken Angelina's life. Perhaps, in view of what had happened, Angelina deserved to die if ever anyone did. Jim Strike was no judge of that. But neither was Arlie Silvershell — nor could he be an executioner. Strike knew he must stop the man. He must not let him murder his wife.

He burst into the street, now filled with people milling about, drawn by the man who owned the buckskin. He would have to rent a horse himself. The bay could not make another hard trip to Tenkiller. Arlie had a good start as it was.

"Jim! Jim!"

He stopped at the summons. It was unmistakably Hannah's voice but what could she be doing there? He turned to look for her.

"Here, Jim — over here!"

She was coming down the street, driving a light buggy. He pushed toward her, shouldering aside those who blocked his path.

He reached the buggy and pulled himself aboard, giving her a tight grin.

"I've been hunting everywhere for you, Jim!" she said in a strained, anxious voice. "I've been so worried."

"Sure glad to see you," he replied and took the reins from her hands.

"I knew you had been hurt," she said, settling onto the seat close to him. "And when you didn't stop and I saw that Arlie Silvershell following you with a gun, I had to come." She paused. "Are you badly hurt?"

He was cutting the buggy sharply about, heading it onto the road. "A scratch. I've got to catch up with Arlie."

"Did he shoot you — in the leg, I mean?"

Strike nodded. There was no time now to tell her everything. He said. "Little misunderstanding we had. I was trying to get away from him before it led to worse trouble. Guess that's all straightened out now, but there's something else. Hannah, he's gone to kill Angelina!"

"Kill her?" Hannah echoed, shocked.

Strike nodded. "He heard some things back there that I tried to make him see this morning. Only he wouldn't believe me. A few minutes ago he found out I was right, that Angelina had been lying to him all along. And carrying on in a way no man could stand for. All his hate has swung to her and unless I can get to him and somehow stop him, he will kill her sure. I know what he's like when he goes wild. He's worse than a crazy man!"

"I saw him — just as I drove into town," Hannah said. "He looked so strange."

They crossed the border and were heading into the town of Long Pass. Strike said, "I'll stop at your place and let you out. Ranch won't be a good place for you to be if trouble starts."

Hannah turned her level gaze to him. "The time for that is gone, Jim, I go where you go."

CHAPTER EIGHTEEN

Angelina moved to the window of the ranch-house parlor and examined her features in a hand mirror. It was a heavy, ivory affair, one of the many pieces that had been in the Mondragon family since the fabulous days of power in far-off Spain. She brushed lightly at the coils of golden hair lying tightly upon her forehead, smoothed her thick, dark brows with an extended forefinger.

After Arlie had departed in such furious haste with the full intention of catching up to and killing his friend, Jim Strike, she had set about dressing for the day. She had chosen a delicate mauve-colored gown, one cut low at the neck, that fitted sleekly along her shapely thighs and then flared to a fullness about her legs. It was a garment that displayed her figure to its best advantage. Just why she had selected that particular dress she had no idea; it was as if the day, begun so brutally, was destined to resolve into one of singular note.

Satisfied with her hair, she applied a small amount of rouge to her lips, dusted her cheeks and slender neck lightly with rice powder. She then added a faint shadowing beneath her eyes. This done, she affixed small jade-and-gold loops to her ear lobes and once again examined her appearance in the glass.

Perfect. She was at her best, she decided. Little wonder she had been able to advance so far with her plans in such short time. She had that commodity most men were willing to pay well for — great beauty. She had used hers well. Her people, she felt, should be most grateful to her.

The door to the hallway opened and Tia Maria entered. In Spanish she said, "It is done, *señora*."

Without turning Angelina asked, "It's all clean? There are no stains anywhere in the room?"

"None," the woman replied in a flat voice. "It was well scrubbed."

"The body?"

"Procopio and Manuel have buried it on the hill."

"Did they fix the door?"

"That, too, is done, *señora*."

She nodded and dismissed the older

woman with a wave of her hand.

It was sad that Pen Moraga was dead. They had made many plans together. They were much alike, knowing exactly what they wanted and not afraid to reach out for it. Pen would have made a good partner and she wished he might have lived until the chore of restoration had been completed. But it did not matter too much. Pen had talked of marriage. But only he had talked of it; it was no thought of hers.

Now it would be necessary to depend upon another man. There were still matters that must be handled. She thought for a moment, culling her mind for a name. Francisco Vaca. He was an old man but faithful to the family. He knew of her plans and was in sympathy with them. He could be depended upon to do her every wish.

She crossed to the hallway and opened the door. "Tia Maria — I wish to talk with Procopio," she called.

She waited there while the aged Mexican shuffled into the room.

"Si, *señora?*"

"Ride to the *mesa* and bring Francisco. I want to talk to him."

"He is not there. He went to Paso Largo. Soon after the *señor* left."

Angelina considered that information for

a moment. She dismissed the old man, returned to the center of the room. Why would Francisco Vaca follow Arlie? He had some thought of aiding him, most likely. Francisco thought well of his master.

She really owed much to Arlie Silvershell. It was he who had built the *hacienda,* the corrals, the barns and other necessary structures. And thanks to his friend, Strike, there were now cattle grazing on the lush green *mesas.* One day they would bring a fine price at the market. And they had cost so little, another favor she owed to poor, dead Pen Moraga and to certain other *Americano* and Mexican ranchers who were willing to pay well for past and future favors.

She stopped, a thought coming to her. Actually, she was ready now to proclaim the rebirth of the Mondragon *hacienda.* She no longer had need for Arlie or any of the others. Perhaps this was to be the day of destiny. She need only to dispatch Procopio to Paso Largo and pass along the word. Immediately the old family *peons,* if they yet lived, or their descendants if they did not, would move back onto the premises and resume their duties as they had in the times long past. Was this then the day? Was that why she had dressed so elegantly?

She walked slowly to the doorway, the

feline gracefulness of her body apparent beneath the sleek covering of her dress. She looked toward the south. Arlie should be returning by this hour. Or perhaps it would be the serious-faced Jim Strike who would come riding in.

It made little difference to her. If Arlie emerged from the affair the victor she would then have no need to fear opposition from Strike and the herd would be unalterably hers. Of course, there would be Arlie to consider, but that was no difficult problem. Jim Strike had answered it himself earlier in the day; an accident. There would be a fall from a horse, perhaps, or a gun being cleaned that went off unexpectedly. It would be simple, logical.

If Strike won out and Arlie were killed, the matter would resolve itself even more easily. Arlie would be out of the way once and for all and Strike, being the sort of man he was, would depart, his type of high-minded conscience and *gringo* principles refusing to allow him to stay on as her partner. It would be nice to have him around for a while — a little while, anyway. Long enough to see if she could break him down.

Someone was coming at last.

She saw him first as a faintly darker

outline far down the valley. It did not appear to be Arlie. This rider was not astride a sorrel horse. Could it be Jim Strike? Her hopes lifted with that thought. If she were to bet on the outcome of gunplay between the two men, she believed she would choose Strike.

It must be Jim Strike, she decided, riding to tell her he had killed Arlie, that she had won out after all. He would tell her he was walking out, leaving it all to her, that he wanted nothing to do with her. She smiled. He would be unaware that such was just what she hoped for. He would be playing straight into her hands. And once he turned and rode out of that yard, the *gringo* ranch of Tenkiller would be dead and the *Hacienda de Mondragon* would live again to rule the valley as of old.

But is was Arlie — not Jim Strike.

She recognized him when he reached the far edge of the watering pond. He was disheveled and he wore no hat, his hair straw-yellow in the sunlight. A measure of her glorious hope fled. It was not to be the great day after all. It was just one more step of accomplishment in the long and tedious restoration of the family crest and position. But it was a large one. It was comforting to know there remained but one more object in the path. Arlie himself.

She watched him circle the water and ride slowly into the yard. He looked very strange, his gaunt face drawn to harsh angles, his eyes pale and empty. He pulled up to the hitching rail on a buckskin horse she never before had seen and dismounted stiffly. She put on her best smile for him, tugged at the collar of the dress and waited. He walked to the porch and halted before her, an odd sort of suppressed tension about him.

"Arlie!" she cried, "Oh, I'm so thankful! I was afraid Strike —"

His voice was like the cutting lash of a rawhide whip. "You lied to me — about everything! You lied — you cheated —"

She fell back under the fury of his words. She stared at him, awed by his appearance and not a little afraid. Before her stood a man she had never known.

"Arlie — you don't believe —" she began. But he slashed though her words.

"Jim Strike was right all the time! I know that now. But I was going to kill him for what he said about you — for what you claimed he did. I know all about you! I talked to Francisco. He told me everything. Even about Pen Moraga — your *cousin!*"

"But he was!" she protested in faint voice. It was incredible. How could things change so quickly? For the first time in her life she was uncertain. "Arlie, I —"

Silvershell shook his head savagely. "I've listened to you for the last time! Once I believed you, everything you told me. I loved you — more than any man should ever love a woman. But it meant nothing to you!" Anger ripped at his features, flared through his eyes. "You ain't fit to live with decent people! You're the worst kind of a killer. You kill everything inside a man and then let him go on living! You tear a man's heart out and throw it down and laugh while you tramp on it! You put a hell right here on earth for him to go through!"

Angelina saw the pistol. She screamed, threw herself back further into the room. The gun roared. Smoke swirled and she felt the scorch of burning powder on her arm. The bullet thudded into the woodwork somewhere beyond her. She screamed again, a high piercing wail. The doorway to the hall was behind her. She flung herself at it, wrenched it open, raced down the short corridor. Behind her the gun crashed once more. A bullet splintered through the panel she had just closed.

She heard Arlie's step in the bedroom, heard him come into the hall. The very silence of the big man was deadly, chilling, like death on the march. She had to keep him from seeing her. Then he could not shoot, could only aim at where he thought she was. There was a loud shattering noise as he booted down the door. Tia Maria cried something from the kitchen but she paid no heed. She had to get away, had to escape and hide where Arlie could not find her.

She burst through the side door into the yard. Manuel, the hostler, attracted by the gunshots, trotted toward her, voicing his question. He could be of no help. She hesitated, thinking of possible safety inside the barn. No, it could easily turn into a trap for her. Arlie would corner her there.

She heard Arlie's heavy tread coming across the kitchen, measured and regular like a drumbeat. He stalked her, like some terrible, wild animal tracking its prey. She looked frantically about, searching for a haven, some sanctuary where he could not reach her.

The canyon.

He would not follow her there. And she knew how to get into it without danger to herself. She would not have to go far into it, where the possibility of slides was the greatest. She needed only to duck into the thick brush and piles of huge rock. Arlie would not follow her. He had always been afraid of it. Quickly she leaped behind one of the small sheds and ran for the shadowy depths of the narrow canyon.

CHAPTER NINETEEN

Hannah and Jim Strike heard the gunshots while they were coming around the watering pond.

Hannah cried, "We're too late!" But a moment later they saw Angelina run into the yard; they watched her pause uncertainly while she sought a place to hide.

They came up to the ranch house at full gallop in time to see Arlie, a huge, vengeful shape, walk resolutely toward the tool shed on the north side of the building where Angelina had taken refuge. Strike pulled their horse to a sliding stop. He leaped from the buggy.

"Wait here," he said to Hannah.

But she did not hear him. She dropped from the vehicle, hurried to keep up with his long strides. They crossed the front of the main house. Somewhere within it Tia Maria's screams were a continuous, shrilling sound. Procopio, with the hostler, was coming from the barn, the ancient muzzle-loading weapon again in his grasp.

Strike looked quickly about for Silvershell. He had been walking toward the shed, but now he was not to be seen. He glanced at Procopio. The old man shook his grizzled head and pointed at the canyon. Strike caught sight of both Angelina and Arlie then. The girl was running, some yards beyond the safety of the fence that had been erected by her husband. She was heading straight into the canyon. Silvershell followed with deliberate, relentless steps.

"Arlie!" Strike yelled and started after the tall Missourian. "Wait!"

If the man heard he paid no heed. He raised his pistol, threw a shot at Angelina. It struck the flat surface of a rock near her, caromed off into the shadows with a high, wailing sound.

The old rifle in Procopio's hands blasted in Strike's ear, almost deafening him. Strike saw Arlie wince and stagger slightly as the ball plowed into his lank body. It did not halt him. He continued on at that deadly, measured pace.

Strike wheeled to the Mexican. "Put that damned thing down!" he snarled and started after Arlie at a run. Then, for the first time, he noticed Hannah at his shoulder. He frowned but said nothing. Together they reached the fence and halted.

"Arlie — listen to me! Don't do this!"

Silvershell pressed on, staggering slightly. He lifted the pistol, held it for a moment to steady his aim. Strike saw a faint splash of lavender in the thick brush and confusion of rocks in the canyon. The gun cracked again. The report slammed about, doubled and redoubled and magnified tremendously between the close, steep walls. A strange, rumbling sound began to rise, to grow.

"Jim!" Hannah cried, turning to Strike. "What is it?"

Angelina burst suddenly from the sheltering brush. Silvershell raised his pistol once more, holding it rigidly with both hands. He sighted carefully. He would not miss this time.

Angelina was coming directly at him, her features strained and pale with fright. Strike heard again that rumbling sound, coming from the deep throat of the canyon. Angelina threw a glance over her shoulder, the long, golden strands of her hair streaming about her. Silvershell heard the earthly thunder also. He lowered his weapon, seemingly brought to some degree of rationality by the awesome noise which was growing steadily in volume.

Understanding came to Jim Strike in that next moment. He yelled his warning.

"Landslide! The gunshots — they've started a slide! Get out of there!"

Suddenly Arlie dropped the pistol. He leaped forward, began to run toward the slender figure scrambling to get clear of the welter of rocks and brush. A shower of gravel and trash began to cascade down around her.

"Angelina!"

Arlie's powerful voice was a piercing summons that struck against the canyon's restless walls. "Angelina — run!"

The girl heard, took courage and started for him, hurrying to reach his outstretched arms as he raced to meet her. Bits of rock and dislodged earth and shattered trees were crashing about her, striking the boulders on the floor of the gash, bouncing crazily away. She tripped, fell prone, scrambled to her feet and rushed on. A branch plunged downward. Its outmost edge caught her, knocked her down. She struggled to an upright position again.

"Angelina — hurry!"

Strike heard Arlie's anguished cry as he plunged into a thickening curtain of rock and earth. The entire valley seemed to shudder. A monstrous roar filled the air. A gigantic plume of dust spewed skyward. A solid wall of rock and debris dropped across the mouth of the canyon. Strike saw Arlie go to his knees as some hurtling object struck him down. But he had reached Angelina. He had gathered her into his powerful arms and pressed her to his chest as if seeking to protect her from the terrible death that had overtaken them both.

They stood in the stuffy lobby of the hotel and waited; Jim Strike, sober-faced and stilled by his thoughts, Hannah close beside him. It was the second day following the deaths of Arlie and his Angelina. They had made their plans and now they were ready to leave.

Strike wanted no more of Tenkiller. There was too much to remind him of Arlie, of Angelina and the past. There must have been some way he could have prevented their tragic ending, he told himself, over and over. But he had not. And now it was too late. Hannah had helped him through those first terrible hours, stayed with him until, at last, he had accepted it. It was finished. They would leave that day. They would be married at the first settlement, since the Shemonites would sanction no union for them. And then they would ride on. Somewhere they would find a place to begin again; a place with no memories.

Standing in the dusty lobby of the hotel, Hannah voiced a question that had bothered her the night before but that she had refrained from asking in deference to the way she knew Jim felt. She moved around to where she faced him squarely and could look into his solemn eyes.

"Jim, I must know this. Perhaps it is a senseless thing, but I will not let it go unanswered until it becomes trouble between us." He returned her gaze. Her blue eyes, in that moment of seriousness, were almost black and her brown hair in its darkness, shone with a high polish. He said, "There can never be anything standing between us, Hannah. Never."

She did not smile. "Jim — were you in love with Angelina?" He stared at her, his features coming alive as disbelief spread through him. A half-laugh, almost a sound of scorn, escaped his lips.

"Love her? Love Angelina? I hated her with everything I had! Not only for what she was, but for what she was doing to Arlie. He was the finest, squarest man I ever knew. Why would you ask such a question of me? How could you think it even likely?"

"Love and hate aren't far apart." Hannah

replied in her quiet way. "Sometimes people mistake one for the other."

"No mistake here," he said softly. "You are the only one — the only one there has ever been or will ever be. I'll tell you that again fifty years from now."

She said, "Thank you, Jim. I needed to hear you say it." She looked away, added thoughtfully, "She was so beautiful. I can understand his feelings for her. Do you think he still loved her — there at the end, I mean?"

He said, "Yes, in spite of all the things she did. Arlie was that way. He went a little crazy when he learned the truth, but when he saw her in danger, about to die, he forgot it all and remembered only how much she meant to him."

Hannah lifted her glance to the doorway. She said, "Here they come, Jim."

Aaron Hendrix's wife was a short woman, thin and careworn and with iron-gray hair. She crossed the lobby to where Hannah and Strike waited, followed by her two sons, both in their early teens.

Strike reached into his pocket and withdrew an envelope. He handed it to the older woman.

"It's all in there, Mrs. Hendrix. Papers that make you legal owner of the ranch. It's yours now. I know it can't begin to make up for Aaron, but at least it gives you a home and a place for the boys."

Mrs. Hendrix accepted the envelope. Her hands trembled and her eyes filled with tears. "I don't know just what to say, Mr. Strike. Nobody's ever done anything kind like this before. And Aaron's always been around to handle such. When you told me about it last night, I just couldn't make myself believe it was so. I still ain't real sure."

"It's true," Hannah said, softly. "Jim wants you and your sons to have it. We're going away."

"But, it's so much!" Mrs. Hendrix said in a faltering voice. "Can't you stay — shouldn't you keep —"

"It's no good to us," Strike broke in. "We've made our plans and nothing can change them. It's the least I can do for Aaron. He was my friend."

"But I —"

"Don't you worry none, Ma," the older boy spoke up. He placed his arm about her frail shoulders. "Joe and me ain't kids no more. We can take care of it."

Jim Strike grinned at the youngster. "You're right, son. You're a man now. You and your brother both. You will make out all right. Good luck."

Hannah linked her arm into his as he wheeled away. He heard her murmur, "Good-by," and together they reached the doorway. Outside the new buggy, loaded with their combined possessions and drawn by the gelding and a matching bay, awaited them.

And a new life lay ahead for them, too. A new and wonderful life, together.

We hope you have enjoyed this Large Print book. Other Thorndike, Wheeler, and Chivers Press Large Print books are available at your library or directly from the publishers.

For information about current and upcoming titles, please call or write, without obligation, to:

Publisher
Thorndike Press
295 Kennedy Memorial Drive
Waterville, ME 04901
Tel. (800) 223-1244

or visit our Web site at:

www.gale.com/thorndike
www.gale.com/wheeler

OR

Chivers Large Print
published by BBC Audiobooks Ltd
St James House, The Square
Lower Bristol Road
Bath BA2 3SB
England
Tel. +44(0) 800 136919
email: bbcaudiobooks@bbc.co.uk
www.bbcaudiobooks.co.uk

All our Large Print titles are designed for easy reading, and all our books are made to last.